Lost in the Tale

Jude Knight

Dedication

To anyone who ever found what they lost, and treasured it all the more.

Come sample my tales

The stories in this book were written as 'Made-to-Order' competition prizes. The winner chose three characters or objects and a story trope. What I did after that was up to me; the raw material of these ideas turned on the lathe of my imagination.

And so you are about to read four short stories and a novella. I offer them as a sample of my writing style, the stories I love to tell, and the types of hero and heroine I love creating. I hope you enjoy getting lost in my tales.

Thank you to Marcia Bucktin, Jennifer Coleman, Dawn Morse, Sheryl Lynne Nyary, and Teri Slabinski Donaldson, who planted the seeds that became these stories.

Table of Contents

The Lost Wife — 1
The Heart of a Wolf — 15
My Lost Highland Lass — 39
Magnus and the Christmas Angel — 67
The Lost Treasure of Lorne — 90
News and special offers — 136
Bluestocking Belles — 136
Published books — 139
Coming in 2017 — 142
Connect with Jude Knight — 145

The Lost Wife

*Teri's refuge had been invaded: by the French, who were trying to conquer their land, and by wounded soldiers from the English forces sent to fight Napoleon's armies. The latest injured man carried to her for nursing would be a bigger challenge than all the rest: he had once broken her heart. (**Short story**)*

Illustration: Head of a Spanish Girl Wearing a Mantilla, ca. 1838 by John Frederick Lewis

1

He was a heavy lad, this Royal Marine. Graham Peters wasn't small himself, and his own wounds were on the mend, or he'd never manage to half drag, half carry the injured captain along the narrow mountain path, barely more than a goat track, that led to the village. He'd been living there for three months, recovering his strength, since a skirmish with the French had left him among the dead beside the road that curved far below them in the valley.

Senorita Bucktin had her usual spies out. A ragged boy popped out from behind a rock, flashed Peters a cheeky grin, and scrambled away up the slope, ignoring the zigzag of the track in favour of the shorter route.

Peters paused for a rest where the path turned, and looked back down to the valley, where the stark detritus of today's battle was made vague by distance. He'd read the signs as well as he could: the lad here would confirm whether or not he was right.

From the looks of it, a French ambush like the one that nearly killed him; this time of a detachment of invalids under a light guard, being sent back from the battle the senorita's roving band of boys had been talking about for the past week.

Control of a fort on the pass at the head of the valley was changing hands back and forth. The British took the fort, then lost it, then took it again. Perhaps they had lost it once more, or perhaps the French marauders that attacked the captain and his column had been trapped on the wrong side of the battle lines.

Certainly, they were not burdening themselves with prisoners. The captain was fortunate his head wound had left him as white and still as death, clearly fooling whoever had been charged with ensuring that no one left the valley alive.

"My men?" The captain asked suddenly, as he had a dozen times already. And Peters answered as he had each time, though the captain clearly did not retain the information. "I'm sorry, captain. You were the only one I found." The only one he had found alive, anyway.

This next bit was the steepest. He looked up at it doubtfully, and was delighted to see the two remaining men who lived in the village making their way down towards him. Jose had only one arm, and Pedro was older than Methusulah, but between the three of them, they could keep the captain on his feet, on the path, and on the climb.

Senorita Bucktin was waiting at the top, where the path more or less levelled for the village square, which was more of a rectangle on two levels. The houses the locals called basseri clung to the hillside above and below, and the most substantial house of the village was at the far end. The senorita's house, and also the village school.

She was some sort of relative of the leader of the band of guerillas that had collected Peters from among the corpses after his own ambush, but had been raised in England, daughter of an English father and Spanish mother. Peters was grateful for that, since he had but a few words of Spanish, and those picked up during the weeks she had nursed him back to health.

"The only survivor?" Senorita Bucktin asked now, but did not wait for an answer. "Bring him this way. I trust you have not strained your shoulder, Sergeant Peters. I will be taking a look at that after I have seen to my new patient. An English soldier, is he?"

"My men?" the captain asked again.

"A British Royal Marine, ma'am. A captain by his rank markings. He is not saying much, ma'am. Fair mazed, he is. Couldn't even tell me his name."

"Captain," Senorita Bucktin said directly to the marine in her clear unaccented English, "we are taking you into the house, and I am going to see to your head. Your rescuer is Sergeant Peters, your helpers are José Garcia and Manuel Ruiz, and I am Senorita Teresa Bucktin."

The captain stopped the determined shuffle that had brought him up from the valley, and for a moment consciousness returned to the one eye showing as he stared at the senorita.

"Teri?" he asked, ducking so he could peer under the hat she wore. Then his eyes rolled up in his head, and he crumpled and would have fallen if Peters hadn't already been half carrying him.

For a moment, Senorita Bucktin froze. She was so white, Peters wondered if she would faint, too. But she shook her head quickly, as if to dislodge something, and began briskly giving orders in both English and Spanish.

Bring the captain inside, Peters understood. Make up a bed. Fetch warm water to bath his wounds, and her medicine chest from her chamber.

2

Teri kept busy. If she were busy enough, she would not have to think. At first, she had seen a patient, not a man. She had focused only on how he let Sergeant Peters take the weight of him: on his wounded head, the bruising, the blood, and the makeshift bandage that concealed one side of the man's face. It was not until she looked into his one light blue eye that she had recognised him.

It could not be David. David was dead. He had disappeared from their hotel a week after their wedding, and his body had been washed up on the shore weeks later. If his best friend, Richard Hemsworth, had not chanced to be in the same town where David left her, who knew what would have become of her? David was dead. Richard had identified the body, and her uncle, David's mother, and Richard's father, the solicitor to whom David had been articled, all assured her it was true. Even if he wasn't dead, he had lied to her—promised that the ceremony in Scotland was a true marriage, when her uncle assured her she could not marry without her guardian's permission.

But in her heart he was her husband still, and that poor foolish organ was hammering with jubilation that he was alive, and fear he would not survive his wounds.

She maintained her outward calm as she washed the wounds. He had been creased by several bullets, and had broken open stitches in his leg from a previous injury. The head injury was the worst of it. Something had blown up close to his head, sending vicious splinters into his face and scalp. She pulled them out one by one: some lumps of steel, some wood. Several of the village women stood by, and held him still whenever he surfaced to something approaching consciousness, but each time the pain sucked him back under.

At first, she thought the eye a bloody ruin, but as she washed away the blood she found he had been unbelievably lucky. No, not lucky. *Thank you, God*, she whispered. *Thank you, David's angel.* And she kept on thanking every saint she could think of, starting with the Blessed Virgin, as she sewed shut the still seeping cuts in and under the brow that had covered him with blood.

It took a long time, and still she was uncertain she had all the splinters. For good measure, she resewed the older wound on his leg. The lesser wounds she left open to the air. The greater wound on his head she spread with a poultice made from mountain lichen and honey, and placed a bandage to protect the poultice and hold it in place.

"Will he live," Peters asked.

"It is in the hands of God, Sergeant Peters," Teri answered. With that in mind, she fetched the rosary that had belonged to her Spanish mother and sat by David's bed to petition Heaven to bestow the gift of life.

In the small hours of the morning, she fell asleep, her head on the bed next to David's hand. She dreamt that they were lying in bed together in the Maryport inn where they spent the week after their wedding at Gretna, talking about their future, David stroking her hair. She woke bereft, as she had at many previous dawns, her heart clenching around her loss and then relaxing again as she remembered the miracle of yesterday. David was alive!

He was still unconscious, however. Teri checked his temperature and his breathing… both normal. Unconscious, or sleeping? Certainly, he'd had the look of an exhausted man, near the end of his endurance.

"Sleeping will help him to heal," she decided. And then what? She still could not comprehend how he could be here, and alive. She went to find Sergeant Peters. He, too, was an early riser, and could be set to watch David while she carried out her duties. There were goats to be milked, bread to set rising, and the children's exercises from yesterday to mark before they arrived for today's classes.

Imanol arrived partway through the second hour of lessons, when the older children were hearing one another read, and she was drilling the younger on their times tables. As usual, he materialised as if by magic, leaning against the wall beside the door.

Teri called the most reliable of the village maidens to take over the arithmetic lesson and went to find out what Imanol wanted, scolding when she found he'd pulled Sergeant Peters from watching the sleeping man. "Head injuries are tricky, Imanol. He cannot be left."

"I needed the skills of the good sergeant, hermanita. The injured man sleeps. And I have work for you, too. Fetch your medicines and bandages, Teresa, and come to the kitchen to see to my men."

She put her hands on her hips and glared at him. "You go watch my patient, and I will deal with your men." Should she tell him the identity of her patient? No. Not until she had been able to talk to David. Then she could decide whether she needed to deal with Imanol's prickly sense of honour and his ideas about what was due to her.

She had three men to treat in the kitchen, one little more than a boy. An encounter with a French patrol, they told her, as she washed and stitched sabre slashes and extracted a bullet from one man's thigh while the others joked about the difficulty he would have sitting.

"And other things," the youngest one said, and collected a buffet from the oldest. "If the Wolf heard you talk like that in front of the senorita, you would never sit again," he growled.

They all called him El Lobo—the wolf. The French had begun it, but the Spanish had picked it up. Senor Juan Imanol Maria Mendina de la Vega, that elegant courtier, was gone—destroyed in the same fire storm that took his jauregi, his mansion, and the grape vines that had been his family's pride. He had brought Teri here to this mountain village, and melted into the mountains with others bent on revenge.

In each of his infrequent visits, he was wilder and more distant. Would the Imanol she loved return when the French were finally driven from these lands? Sometimes, she feared he was gone forever.

3

David surfaced slowly from a dream in which he had returned to his home village and found Teri gone. He lay with his eyes shut, waiting for the surge of grief to subside. Every time he had that dream, the pain was rawly new, all the more real for being a memory. He had no idea how he'd come to be in the ocean, but the sharp-eyed sailor who saw him, and the captain who ordered him fished aboard, had his gratitude, even if they would not turn back to return him to shore.

He worked his passage to the Azores, then found another boat and worked his way home, all the while expecting his wife to be waiting with her mother or his until he returned.

She was gone. Her mother had died, and Teri had run off with another man, his mother told him. He could not believe it, but everyone in the village told the same tale, even Richard, who had been his dearest friend until they both fell in love with the same woman. Even Teri's own uncle.

Somewhere, deep down, he still did not believe it, and she filled his dreams night after night, though ten years had passed. She even invaded his delirium, for he vaguely remembered a pain-filled clamber up mountains, a giant of a man with a soothing lowland Scots burr, and Teri, waiting for him at the end of the climb. And again, in the night, he could swear he'd woken and stroked her silk-soft hair, stray wisps that had escaped her tight plait clinging to his fingers as they had in that one blissful week of marriage.

His head hurt like the devil, and his throat felt as if his entire regiment of marines had tramped through it with sandy boots. If he was in a hospital, it smelt like no hospital he'd ever entered: crisp clean linen and fresh mountain air. Had they brought him to a convent?

David opened one eye, cautiously. He was in a whitewashed room, sparsely furnished. Everything from the deeply recessed window with the arched top to the tiled floor to the brightly-coloured hand-crafted spread to the gaudily painted crucifix on the wall suggested he was still in the mountains between Spain and Portugal. A dark man with a thin face and neatly trimmed beard lay at his ease on the other bed, his hands behind his head and his near-black eyes watching David thoughtfully.

"Water?" David's voice came out in a croak, and the man unfurled and crossed unhurriedly to a jug on a table beside the bed before David had time to think that he should have asked in Spanish.

He tried to sit up, but the man scolded. "No, no. Let me help, English. If I let you open your wounds *mi hermanita* will be cross."

David subsided, more from lack of strength than from compliance, and the man supported his head while David sipped, absorbed in the small miracle of the liquid sliding over the parched surfaces and soothing them.

"My men?" he asked, when he could speak. Not just the small company of marines, all with some injury, that he took to defend the cartloads of wounded, but all the injured men for whom he had been responsible. All gone? All?

He had asked the giant, too, he remembered, and this man gave him the same answer.

"I am sorry, English. The good Sergeant Peters found only you alive."

In the cruel economy of war, only a fool left living enemies behind him, and a band scrabbling for survival in this unforgiving landscape could not afford prisoners. Both sides made the same cold calculations, but still, the massacre of a baggage train of wounded men turned David's stomach.

"Murdering bastards," he said, and this fetched a nod from the Spaniard—or was he Portugese? Could be either this close to the border.

"Their time in these mountains is short," the man consoled. "We are taking one fort after another with the help of you English. And we will hunt down the 'murdering bastards' to the last man."

"But I forget my manners." The man drew himself up and bowed with an elegance that was ill-suited to the peasant clothing he wore, though his flair transmuted it into something more appropriate to a gentleman.

"I am Imanol Mendina de la Vega. Welcome to my humble residence, and that of my *hermana*."

Hermana. He had said something similar earlier. Long ago, David had learnt a little Spanish to please Teri's Mama, stranded as she was as a widowed Spanish lady in the very English household of her brother-in-law. But he did not know that word.

He shifted his head on the pillow, the closest he could come to a bow. "David Markinson, Captain of His Majesty's Royal Marines."

Something fierce suddenly surfaced in Imanol's dark intent eyes. "Markinson? Is that a common name in England?"

"Not particularly. It is more common in Scotland. My family are border people."

"Border? Ah. Between two kingdoms. And what is the name of this border town you come from, Captain Markinson?"

"Blackwood," David said. Once he had thought to spend all his days there; to take his articles with his employer, Mr Hemsworth, to raise a family of children with Teri and grow old in a cottage with roses around the door. After his dreams turned to dust, he had enlisted with the marines, and his mother's death two years ago severed his last links to the place.

Imanol was scowling, his heavy brows nearly meeting above the bridge of his nose, but his voice, courteous and calm, showed none of the emotion written on his face. "And have you a wife back there in Blackwood, captain? Or a girl who loves you, perhaps?"

"No." Not that it was any of this man's business. "Not anymore. I have no-one." *I have a wife somewhere,* his heart protested. *Not back there in Blackwood,* he answered his own objection.

Imanol opened his mouth to say something more, then turned to the door and fell silent.

David shifted his head on the pillow, but couldn't turn it enough to see who stood there; who was asking a peremptory question in Spanish that was too fast for him to follow. A woman's voice, and

Imanol did not like what she said, for his answer was sharp. They argued for a few minutes more, and David tried still harder to see the woman. He could swear he knew the voice.

The altercation ended with Imanol saying to David, "Be careful, English. She says I must not gut you like a fish, but she does not rule here." Another sentence or two in Spanish, and he left. David lay back, waiting, and sure enough the woman came into the room where he could see her. It was her. Older. In the clothes of a village woman rather than those of an English lady. But it was Teri. Maria Teresa Markinson, his runaway wife.

While he gaped, lost for words, she rested the back of her hand on his forehead, and picked up his wrist to feel for his pulse. "How is the head?" she asked. "Do you feel any pull from the stitches?"

David grabbed the hand before she could remove it. "Teri." He struggled to order his thoughts, but they slithered out his grasp and he could only cling to her hand as if she anchored him to reality instead of driving him out of his mind.

"Take your hand off her." Imanol's cold voice gave David words.

"She is my wife!" he declared at the same moment that Teri said, "Go away, Imanol."

"Your abandoned wife," Imanol sneered.

"No! Is that what you thought, Teri? No. I did not leave you. Not by my choice."

He had both hands now, but Teri had turned so pale he thought she might faint. Imanol must have thought so, too, for he came into sight, fetched a chair from the table under the window, and set it so that Teri could sit down.

"Perhaps I will not gut you yet, English. Not until you have explained. Ask your questions, Teresa." He stood with one hand on Teri's shoulder, and met David's glare with a slight smile.

"She is my wife," David said again, stressing the word *my*.

"They said we were not married." Teri's words were so quiet he had to strain to hear them. "They said I could not wed without my uncle's consent, and so our marriage was not valid. They said you must have known. Well, that is true, you were training to be a solicitor, so how could you not know?"

David was shaking his head. "Lies. All lies. Who told you such lies? That is why we went to Scotland, Teri. I told you, remember?

Your uncle would not consent to our marriage, and in Scotland we did not need his consent. We were married. We are married."

Teri was nodding. "They lied," she confirmed, and she turned and looked up at Imanol. "They lied to me, Imanol. They said he was dead."

"Who is this 'they'?" David demanded.

"My uncle. Your mother. Mr Hemsworth. Richard."

"They told me you had left; run away with another man. And here you are," he glared at the Spaniard, "with him. Why did you not wait, Teri?"

Teri was shaking her head, tears filling her eyes, and it was Imanol who spoke. "For what, English, and how? Those she trusted said you were dead and a liar besides. Her mother had died, and your own turned her out when she refused to marry this oh so noble friend of yours. This Richard."

David, his mind reeling, had no words. All he could do was shake his head and hold onto Teri's hands, a grip she was now returning as if determined never to let him go again. His poor love. Abandoned and betrayed, or so she thought, then left alone with no one to turn to.

"How did you come to leave," Imanol asked. The hostility was gone from the Spaniard's voice, but David could hear it in his own as he told Teri, not the man who had taken her away.

"You remember I went to hire a post chaise for our return journey? The last thing I remember is going into the inn yard. When I was next aware, I was on a ship on my way to the Americas. They fished me from the sea, Teri, and I have no idea how I came to be there. I persuaded them to land me at San Miguel, the first place we stopped, but it took time to find a ship heading for England that would take me, and we hit heavy weather. I came as fast as I could, Teri." He clutched her hands convulsively as he relived the moment when his mother told him 'the Spanish whore has gone with one of her own kind, and good riddance'.

"I don't understand." Teri still drew her brows into a kissable crease when she was puzzled. "Richard asked all over Maryport. And then he went back to identify your body after it was washed up by the sea."

"Richard? He went to Maryport to find me?"

"I don't know what I would have done without him. You had our money, David. If Richard had not turned up that same night, I would have been at a stand."

David met Imanol's eyes over Teri's head. Richard. Richard was at every turn of this tale. Rescuing the abandoned wife. Consoling the grieving widow. Offering for the ruined orphan.

"And does he yet live in this village, *hermano*?" Imanol's voice was soft but lethally sharp, and Teri turned to him, startled.

"You do not think… but Richard was David's friend!"

Imanol gestured with his head, and she turned to David, who nodded. "He wanted you, Teri. But I never thought he would stoop to murder and lies. In the end, though, even with me out of the way, you did not choose him." That would explain the invective Richard heaped on her when David returned, words that broke what was left of their friendship and ceased only when David stopped the traitor's mouth with his fist.

If he had known then…

"He enlisted with the dragoons and died last fall," David told Imanol.

"It is for the best," Imanol reassured him. "For honour would demand satisfaction, and there is the small matter of the French at present. All is well, then Teresa. I will leave you with your *esposo* and away to my men. Perhaps I will see you on my next visit, *hermano*. Be good to her or I shall gut you yet." His dark eyes gleamed with humour as he pushed away from the chair.

"Just like that?" The Spaniard was leaving the field to David? "Wait. What does it mean, '*hermano*'?"

The corner of Imanol's mouth quirked upwards at that, but he slid out of the room without comment.

"Brother," Teri said. "It means 'brother'. Imanol is my mother's son by her first marriage." She pulled back, mock indignant. "What did you think, David? That I had run off with another man?

He could have said that she had thought him false and a liar, but a week of marriage was enough to give him a small measure of wisdom, and instead he changed the subject. "Come here and give me a kiss, Teri. For I lost you, and now I have found you, and we have ten lost years for which to make up."

4

Graham Peters had rejoined his regiment in Santander, recently liberated from the French. He'd been absent in the mountains for months, at first recovering, then supporting the guerillas. And his general was delighted with his work, and was sending him back up into the mountains. Just as well. He no longer had the shoulder strength to manage the work he had once done so easily, but he had become skilled at the repairs El Lobo needed to keep his equipment and his wiry mountain ponies functioning.

Captain and Mrs Markinson were taking ship to England from the Santander port—Mr Markinson, rather, for the thigh wound had turned putrid and—though Mrs Markinson's devoted care saved the leg—Markinson would walk with a pronounced limp for the rest of his life.

Peters would miss the Markinsons. He had moved out of the main house after Markinson got back together with his bride, but he still saw them daily. Indeed, when Markinson was at his sickest, Peters had taken over the school so Mrs Markinson could nurse her husband. A fine hash he made of it, but the children learned a little English, and he a little Spanish.

It had taken months before Markinson had been up and about again, though Mrs Markinson's silhouette hinted that he'd had energy enough for his bride.

Markinson was a lucky man, Peters thought, going home to England with a wife, a child on the way, and the promise of a new career in law. El Lobo had a friend who was a solicitor in London, and who had agreed to take Markinson on. "Take *mi hermana* away from this war, English," he commanded.

And so now Peters and El Lobo stood shoulder to shoulder watching the Markinsons being rowed out to the ship that would take them home, and climbing up the side, Mrs Markinson a little ungainly already with the coming child.

Mrs Markinson waved towards the shore, and Peters waved back. After a moment, El Lobo raised one hand in a lordly sweep across the air, then turned away.

"Come, Sergeant Peters. We have a war to win, you and I."

THE END

The Heart of a Wolf

Ten years ago, Isadora lied to save her best friend, and lost her home and the man she loved when he would not listen to her. Ten years ago, Bastian caught his betrothed in the arms of another man, and her guilt was confirmed when she fled. A decade on, anger still burns over the embers of their love, but the lives of innocent children and the future of their werewolf kind demand that they work together. (Short story)

1

Sebastian drove the horse hard. The best the posting inn had to offer, it was still a poor specimen compared to those in his own stables, but even his best stallion could not have outrun the temper that burned within.

Nathaniel dead. That Woman's husband with him. Sebastian left with a letter from his brother, hand delivered by a solicitor so that Sebastian could not consign it to the fire as he had all its predecessors. And with it came a charge he wanted to repudiate with all his considerable power. Responsibility for the protection of That Woman and her brats? How could Nathan demand that of him, given what she had done?

But the letter claimed she had been innocent all those years ago. He stiffened in denial, and the horse responded to the sudden pressure on its flanks with a burst of desperate speed, struggling up the hill that lay between him and his goal.

No. He knew what he had seen: his betrothed, barely out of the schoolroom, her virginal white dress crumpled and pulled down from one shoulder, her hair disordered and her face white with shock and strain at being discovered. Jeremy Harris, Nathan's tutor, in worse disarray, hastily rebuttoning his fall. And Nathan, the greatest betrayal of all. His beloved brother interposing his body between the guilty couple and Sebastian, stammering something Sebastian could not hear because of the roaring of the beast.

The beast stirred within him now, restive at the thought of at last having power over the woman it had claimed long ago. She had been ten years old, and he a young man of twenty, but the beast within had recognised something that only those of the old blood could detect; like calling to like. She carried the magic. He had, then and there, negotiated with the baron her father, and carried her off as his affianced bride to be raised with his own brother.

Seven years of patiently waiting for her to grow. Seven years of giving her a little more of his heart every day. Seven years of training her to be his duchess and his queen.

At first, the call had been spirit to spirit, but as she grew into young womanhood, he fell in love, deeply and irretrievably. He thought she had done the same. He rejoiced in the vision of a golden future, for them and their people.

Lost in one evening. Had it not been for Nathan, he would have killed them both: Isadora and her lover.

He took a deep breath, fighting to reassert his iron control; the horse was near to outright panic, and he had no wish to destroy an innocent animal.

"Easy, fellow. Easy," he crooned. To himself or to the horse, he hardly knew. He would need to calm himself before he could exert his will in the other gift bestowed by the old blood. Though, in truth, the ability to control the minds of others was a characteristic of his beast rather than a separate ability.

The horse surged over the hill, and there below he could see the remote estate to which the guilty couple had fled, taking Sebastian's only brother with them. No more of these thoughts. He turned the horse to follow the winding path down to the flats, encouraging it to slowly easy its speed, and he was halfway down the hill before he had attention to pay to the scene below.

The sounds of which he had barely been aware—the screaming of a mob out for blood—were not his own angry thoughts, but came from the valley. There. In the distance beyond the house. People on horseback followed by others on foot, all pursuing… what? Too big for foxes. Dogs?

He leaned a little of the beast into his nostrils, and the scent carried on the wind told him the whole story. Wolves. Two juveniles. Wolves in England in the 19th Century. And wolves, furthermore, that reeked of the old blood. It could mean only one thing.

His body had reacted before his mind, his heels spurring the horse into one last effort, plunging madly down the hill, over a fence, across a ditch, up a haha, and across the lawn towards the house.

The wolves had a one-hundred-yard lead on their pursuers, and as Sebastian closed on the house from the front, they approached from the side. A howl from the mob almost drowned the sound of several shots. What were the fools thinking, to fire on the house? One of the wolves faltered as the other leapt for a window, then the laggard followed. Sebastian pulled his horse to a trembling stop and took the steps to the main door of the house in a leap, crashing inside and pushing past the servant who tried to stop him, backing the physical shove with a mental push and a ducal glare.

He did not need to ask which room. The middle of the three doors to the right side of the entrance hall reeked of the old magic. Sebastian burst into the parlour beyond and stopped.

It was her. That woman. Isadora Harris. The traitor bride and widow of the traitor tutor. He noted at a glance that she had more than fulfilled her early promise of great beauty, but most of his attention was on the two with her. One was a boy of eleven or twelve whose naked body bore clear signs of neglect and abuse: the coppery brown skin stretched over protruding bones, new bruises and whip cuts layer upon layer over the scars of old. The other huddled at Isadora's feet, a young she-wolf, her amber eyes glazed with pain, blood matting the fur of her shoulder.

For a moment, the three froze in a tableau, Isadora's hands out to comfort and protect the ill-assorted pair. Then all changed before his eyes. The boy was suddenly well fed and clean, dressed in a sturdy suit of nankeen, his skin several shades lighter and his nose and lips narrower. And where the wolf had been, a girl sat at Isadora's feet, her long black hair in a plait down her back, her modest school-girl dress the same shade of amber as her eyes had been an instant before. They were brown now, but still fixed on Isadora with the same silent plea.

2

He had come. Sebastian Marrock, the high and mighty Duke of Bleidrich. Lord Pomp and Arrogance himself. After ignoring all of Nathan's other letters, when it was too late to make peace with his brother, he turned up at their door. And at just the wrong moment, too, when the mob she could hear outside was beginning to invade her house, in search of the children she would die to protect.

Isadora had no time for His Self-Righteousness at the moment. She focused all of her awareness on what she wanted the intruders to see, pouring her life energies into an illusion that would fool them as long as she could keep them from touching. It wasn't a true change, but it would serve.

"Be still, Mei Ling," she told her adoptive daughter. As far as she could see, the bullet had just grazed the skin. She hoped there was no deeper wound, for she must repel the invaders before she could check the injuries—Mei Ling's and those of the stranger Mei Ling had rescued. "Don't move, young man. Let me get rid of those who pursue you, and then we shall talk, yes?"

The boy, his eyes wild, looked up from the suit of clothes that had suddenly appeared on his body, and considered her gravely, then darted a sideways look at the duke before nodding, warily.

She could not answer for the duke. Nathan had been certain his brother would welcome the little tribe he and Jeremy had gathered in their travels: twenty-three girls and boys—twenty-four now— whose remote ancestors had bequeathed them the power to change into wolves and had thereby placed them in great danger when the power came on them of a sudden, and the ungifted around them sought to kill what they did not understand.

But the Duke of Blindness had been quite clear when he had plucked her from her home as a child. He had sifted the nobility, looking for a bride whose blood called to his, starting with his ducal peers and moving down the ranks until he found her near the bottom of those whose existence he deigned to recognise.

The children Nathan and Jemmy saved had been found among the poorest of the poor; people who were beneath His Gracelessness's notice.

Surely, even if he would not claim them as pack, he would not throw them to the mob that was tramping down her hall, arguing loudly with her butler?

The door crashed back against the wall, and several men tried to struggle through the frame at once, all shouting invective until the duke shouted, "Quiet!"

The boy flinched and Isadora tightened her hand on his shoulder.

"How dare you! How dare you break into a lady's home, abuse her servants, shoot at her windows, damn you! I should have you all taken in charge!"

The angry duke was a magnificent sight, Isadora could concede when the anger was not addressed at her, and it was working on its targets, who had shrivelled at the duke's onslaught. She recognised them, had done business with most of them: Mr Mason, the baker; Mr Williams, one of the most prosperous small-holders in the district; Metcliffe, Master of Hounds to the squire; and over their shoulders the Rev'd Clarkson, three more farmers, and several other merchants and tradesmen of the town, all looking awkward and shamefaced as the duke continued his tirade.

She did not know the man who was now pushing his way into the room, a small wiry man with tiny mean eyes and the sharp face of a weasel. His voice, truculent and defiant, betrayed his uncertainty where the words didn't. "I dunno 'oo you be, and I don't care. I wants my boy, and I seen 'im jump in that there window. So 'and 'im over and the other one wot stole 'im."

Isadora opened her mouth to argue, but shut it at a glare from His Gracelessness. Very well. She would leave it to him. He seemed, at least, to be taking their part.

The duke lowered his voice, and the resulting low calm tones were somehow more terrifying than his shout, a sort of purring growl full of menace. "I am, you ill-mannered cur, the Duke of Bleidrich, guardian of the children in this house, and the betrothed of Lady Isadora, the lady you are so offending with your dangerous and insane pursuit. A boy, you say?" He edged his words with contempt, and the Rev'd began to inch away towards the back of the crowd. "I saw a pack of heathen savages after a pair of foxes, or perhaps dogs. I saw no boy."

"Not dogs," the man told him, standing his ground. "The boy turns into a wolf. I seen it myself, many times. These people. They seen it too." He turned to his allies. Several had slipped away from the rear, and none of the others would meet his eyes.

"Ah, I see," the duke said, raising his chin, his nose, and a pair of lofty brows in lordly disdain. "A showman, I take it?" This was addressed to Williams, who looked to his fellows before admitting, "Yes, my lord. 'E is. Not from around 'ere, my lord."

"The correct form of address is 'Your Grace'," the duke explained, not unkindly.

Isadora was pouring all her strength into holding the illusion, but a small part of her mind noted and appreciated how he was playing this crowd.

"Your Grace," Williams repeated, humbly.

"I see your game," the duke told the showman. "You have some trick for switching the dog and the boy to gull money from our good people here. And then your dog escaped and you saw the chance of some other scheme, I do not doubt. Well, I have no problem with you recapturing your poor animal. But not in this lady's house. You can see for yourself, there are no dogs here."

"It ain't none of it true," the showman insisted. "The boy turns into a wolf. And I seen 'im myself jump in that there window."

Isadora had never realised what a showman the Duke of Bleidrich was. With a long-suffering sigh, and a look of commiseration at Williams, he turned to Isadora. "My lady," he said, his voice heavy with patience. "Did you perchance see a dog, or a wolf, or any other kind of animal jump in the window behind you?"

"I did not," said Isadora, truthfully, since her back had been to the window all along. For good measure she added, "No one has been in this room this last hour but myself and the children, until you and these gentlemen arrived.

The duke turned back to his audience, which was significantly smaller now, most of those who could not get into the room having made their escape. "There you have it. Good day to you. I suggest the beasts must have slipped along the side of the house and will now be well on their way to the next county."

With bows, and apologies, and much muttering from the showman, the remaining villagers took themselves off.

As soon as she heard the front door shut behind the last of them, Isadora let slip the threads of the illusion, and sat back against her cushions, her eyes shut, momentarily limp with exhaustion.

3

Sebastian followed the mob out into the hall and watched as they left, one by one, using a touch of the coercive power that was his gift to speed them on their way. The servant closed the door almost on the heels of the sullen showman, who was being assisted from the premises, none too gently, by two of the local people.

Sebastian turned from the door and beheld riches. Spread down the stair, in a variety of sizes and colours; boys and girls; every skin tone from palest English cream to ebony black; the youngest perhaps seven or eight and the oldest in his mid-twenties. They all bore the tempting odour of the old blood. And—except for the youngest—every pair of eyes fixed warily on Sebastian was silver, amber or deep emerald, the tell-tale sign of one who had changed.

"I leave you my treasures, Bastian," Nathan's letter had said. "I have made you guardian of the younger ones, but you will want all of our children and won't care a bit where they came from."

All of them. A score or more, and Nathan was right, too, when he said that Sebastian would not care about their origins. Sebastian had read that wrong, had assumed Nathan was making him guardian of Isadora's children, had jumped to scandalous conclusions about the relationship between Nathan, Harris, and Harris's wife.

These children were too old and too diverse for Isadora to have birthed, and if they came from the sewers and gutters of all Europe, Sebastian did not care. They bore the old blood. More, they were strong enough in the blood that they could change. Treasures indeed.

His fiercely possessive grin broke the tableau, the oldest of the young men moving through the crowd on the stairs asking, "What has happened? is it Mei Ling?"

Sebastian, recalled to the young wolf's need, made for the parlour, reaching the door just ahead of the young man and the servant, but they followed hard on his heels as he entered the room, and the youngest child, a little Asian boy, squirmed through their legs and under their arms to throw himself beside the wolf.

"Mei Ling!" he cried, then looked piteously up at Isadora. "Mama? Is Mei Ling dead?"

Isadora was half-fainting on the couch, so drained of colour and energy that a thin tracery of blue veins showed on her drawn brow, but she roused at that, saying, in little more than a croak, "Just tired, Ping Ping." The wolf, too, made an effort, opening her eyes and whimpering a little, so that the boy lay his head on the floor beside hers and cuddled into the soft fur.

Sebastian had seen exhaustion such as Isadora's on those who had spun their own life reserves into whatever magic was their gift. "Bring food for your lady, and a nourishing drink," he commanded the servant. I will see to the girl; Mei Ling, is it? And this other?" He looked his question to the young man from the stairs. The others seemed well cared for—nourished, not visibly abused.

"Beef tea, Barrett, and some of the meat pie. Perhaps some biscuits," the young man commanded. "Clara, fetch a blanket for Mei Ling, and a medical kit to see to her wounds, and those of the stranger." Sebastian almost said he had no wounds, but the stranger was the naked boy, of course.

His commands given and swiftly obeyed, the young man addressed himself to Sebastian. "I do not know who you are, Sir, but I can care for those in my charge." He met Sebastian's glare, his only sign of unease a tension in his neck and flaring of nostrils.

Such courage deserved to be rewarded with an introduction. "I am the Duke of Bleidrich, guardian to these children by my brother's charge, and King to them and to you by my blood and my power." He threw a little of his coercive will at the impudent fellow, and was perversely pleased when the only response was a slight waver in the voice that said. "I am Christopher Harris, Your Grace, tutor to these children."

A relative of the infamous Jeremy Harris, Nathan's tutor, who had stolen the affections of Sebastian's bride and Sebastian's brother? Or another rescuee? Time enough to explore that question later.

"The boy looks to have taken no new hurt, but these cuts and bruises will need care. Lady Isadora will recover with food and sleep. Let me look at this young lady." He knelt beside the wolf, and she turned her pain-hazed eyes trustfully to him. "Do not be afraid, Mei Ling. I need to see if the bullet is still in the wound, and if there are other injuries, but I think you are more tired and frightened than injured." He went on talking as his hands gently smoothed over the wolf's pelt, and felt around the wound, mostly to calm the boy Ping Ping, who was soon leaning against him and watching his eyes as he spoke.

Around him, he was aware of others moving in and out of the room. Isadora was helped to sit up on the couch, propped on cushions, and one of the girls sat feeding her sips of beef tea from a spoon until she had recovered enough to take a little biscuit. A group of boys had wrapped the stranger in a blanket and led him away. Young Harris squatted on his haunches next to Sebastian, passing whatever was needed: a bowl of water and a cloth, a towel, a bandage. Thankfully, the wound was just a graze, and he did not need to remove a bullet.

"A dressing would be easier, Mei Ling, if you take your human form," he coaxed.

"Not in the same room as all you men," Isadora told him, scornfully, her voice sounding slightly stronger.

Ah. Of course. When she lost the fur of her wolf form, Mei Ling would be naked.

"We will take her now, Your Grace, Chris," said the young woman Harris had called Clara. She had organised the medical supplies Harris had asked for, and was now waiting with a makeshift stretcher: a pallet covered in a blanket, with a girl on each corner to carry it.

Sebastian shook his head when Harris went to lift Mei Ling, performing that office himself, settling her tenderly on the blanket and rubbing a wondering hand over the miracle of her wolf's head. "Be at ease, little one," he told Ping Ping. "Your sister shall be well."

The little boy trotted off after the stretcher crew, and Sebastian was free to turn his attention to Isadora. She had recovered enough to be eating ravenously. He had seldom seen anyone so drained and he was relieved that her skin appeared less stretched over her bones, the colour returning to her face.

A memory assailed him. This same woman, ten years younger, but in the same state of exhaustion, half drooping, held up by Harris on one side and Nathan on the other. On the night of their betrothal ball, at the scene of her disgrace. At the time, he'd thought her afraid and embarrassed, but that extreme a reaction? In one who defied him and left that same night? Had she cast an illusion that night, and if so why? And of what?

A knock on the front door had him reaching for his sword stick. Harris moved to his right shoulder and another younger man to his left, sending a surge of pride through Sebastian. They acknowledged him as their king whether they knew it yet or not.

He gestured the stand-down when he heard the voice at the door. Thomas, his secretary, cousin, and sometime valet, when travel meant they needed to make do. Thomas was not able to change. The old blood in him manifested in one gift, and that a small one. Where Sebastian could smell a difference in those who bore the old blood, Thomas could see it. A light, he said. An aura around all living things, and those of the old blood shining more brightly than their merely human fellows. Thomas could even predict with considerable accuracy which gifted youngling would succumb to the change after they reached puberty.

A small gift, but very useful. Thanks to Thomas, Sebastian knew that none of his daughters would change. The blood was thin in them as it had been in their mother, his cousin Greville's daughter, Alice. But with Isadora gone, he had been desperate to produce offspring to lead his pack, and perhaps if he wed each of the girls to one of the few changers he had left, he might yet breed a grandson who could be a true Duke of the Wolf Kingdom, which is what his title meant in the tongue of the people who once ruled this land.

Or, he thought, with rising hope, glancing at the tired woman who glared resentfully at him from the couch, perhaps he could return to his first choice. For he was now a widower, and she a widow. Further, he had already claimed her as betrothed in front of witnesses and she had not gainsayed him. In some places, that would be enough to bind them for life.

Innocent, Nathan had claimed, and he had refused to listen. Had he been blinded by his hurt and pride? But she had not waited to explain. She had fled. Still… innocent? He could not see how, but he longed to be convinced.

Thomas entered the room, his mouth agape. "This place shines like the sun, Your Grace. The auras, they…" he stopped, abashed at the room full of people.

"Lady Isadora, allow me to present my graceless cousin Thomas Maddock. Harris, my cousin Maddock. Harris is Lady Isadora's lieutenant, I collect, Thomas. Come. Let us leave my lady to her rest. Harris, would you be good enough to take us to the schoolroom and introduce us to the rest of my wards? And tell me their names and ages as we go, if you please."

4

The Duke of Arrogance did not ask questions. He made pronouncements, and those around him scurried to please him. The room emptied, and Isadora could hear Christopher answering the duke as they climbed the stairs.

She should be pleased he had so readily accepted the children. Instead, she felt a vast, weary resentment. Relief, yes. The locals had become more and more suspicious of the growing family at the big house. And today's incident would raise the level of hostility even after Bleidrich's intervention. If the duke had not arrived, they might now all be dead or fleeing.

But the debt made her resentment greater. Why could he not have come earlier? Ten years! Ten years of letters from Nathan and silence from his brother. Ten years of comforting her best friend in the world, and abetting his every effort to realise the duke's vision without any acknowledgement or assurance that the duke would be pleased.

Chris had been the first, rescued from a lockup in a village where they stopped at on their way into exile after the disaster that her betrothal ball had become. The change had come upon Chris without warning, when all memory of the old blood had been lost in his family. Every time he lost his temper he slipped into wolf form. He would have been shot before Nathan and Jemmy could buy him free, if the county constable had not been a rationalist who refused to believe his own eyes.

Slowly, person by person, their band grew, until Jemmy and Isadora were as enthusiastic as Nathan in the search for those rejected from their families, their communities, when the change came on them. The children of workhouses, farmyards, slum tenements; young traders and farmers and servants; travellers and fishermen—all surprised by the consequences when two random descendants of straying young wolf warriors chanced to meet and to concentrate the ancient inheritance in the bloodline.

Go away! she wanted to scream at His Ungraced. You didn't care about your brother while he lived. You cannot take the children now!"

But fortunately, she was too tired to argue. For he would take the children, whether she objected or not, and they would be better off if he did. Damn the man to perdition and back.

She let her eyes close. Best that she sleep. Undoubtedly, His Child-Stealing Impudence would be back, and she needed her strength to deal with him, and the stupid feelings that a decade of silence had not killed. She still loved him. How stupid.

She barely stirred when they moved her to her bed; when her maid removed her dress and jumps, and slipped a nightrail over her head; when her adoptive daughters tucked the blankets around her chin and kissed her cheek.

She slept, and woke, and ate, and slept again. Vaguely, she remembered this bone-deep exhaustion. She had lost most of the carriage ride that had been their flight into exile, sleeping off the effects of the illusion that had saved Nathan and Jemmy.

Clara was beside her when she finally woke refreshed. From the light in the room, it was late afternoon. Clara looked up from the breeches she was mending—a houseful of boys makes for a powerful lot of mending—and smiled. "You are awake at last, Dorrie. Uncle Bastian said it would be this evening. He said to tell you that he left it to your judgement whether you came down to dinner or had it served to you here."

Uncle Bastian? And giving orders about her dinner? Well, not orders, precisely, but saying he would leave it to her judgement was bad enough, implying that his judgement would prevail but for his oh so gracious condescension.

Clearly, he had wormed his way into her children's esteem while she had been asleep, and now he would think to run her household. He had called her Lady Isadora, his betrothed, she remembered.

Well. She would soon disabuse the pompous arrogant numbskull of that notion.

But her head swam a little when she went to sit up, and she would need to be at her best to deal with the Duke of Presumption, especially in front of the household he had clearly seduced to his side.

"I will eat here, Clara," she told her foster-daughter and friend, "and will come down to breakfast tomorrow. Now tell me about Mei Ling and the boy she rescued."

5

Isadora was awake, and looking well, Clara said, but would eat in her room. Sebastian had expected it, but still felt a crashing sense of disappointment. His long anger was dissolving in bewildered embarrassment. Everything he had learned since he arrived in the house a day and a half ago confirmed his sense that he'd made a fundamental error ten years ago and compounded it ever since. He had been wrong, and he hated being wrong.

He still did not know what had really happened the night of his betrothal ball, but he no longer doubted those few casual words in Nathaniel's letter: "…and you will not deny your protection to my dear Dorrie, for you know she was an innocent of all that was said against her."

He would deny Isadora nothing, but he still needed to understand, and she was the only person who could explain. His own stubbornness and the accident that took Nathan and Harris had robbed him of the other two who knew the whole story.

He left the younger people to their conversation and made his way up to the suite assigned to him. The Master's room, Barrett had told him. Nathan's or Harris's? Harris's, he supposed. The children all took Harris as a surname. It hardly mattered, and he hadn't asked.

Isadora's room was on the same floor. No connecting door, oddly, and down a short passageway. He found himself outside the door, told himself someone should check to see if she had everything she needed. Nonsense. He just wanted to see her.

She was sitting on the window seat, looking out into the garden, but she turned and glared as he entered the room.

"You should not be here."

"I needed to see for myself that you were recovered," he explained, oddly uncomfortable.

"Well. You have seen. You can go." And she turned back to the window, muttering in a voice that was meant to be too low to hear, "Because far be it from His Grace the Duke of Omniscience to believe anyone else's witness."

His hearing was unusually keen, even in human form. "The duke is not nearly as all-seeing as he once thought," he told her. She had a right to an apology, but he would like some idea of the size of his offence before he offered it.

His unusual humility met an unexpected response. She whirled back and advanced on him, high spots of colour on her cheeks and her eyes bright. "I am so, so angry with you, Your Grace."

He backed up a step, wary, though not unaware of how magnificent she looked in her rage.

"I am sorry?" he offered.

"Ten years! Ten years, Bleidrich. He loved you so much, and you ignored him for ten years. He lived, breathed, worked to find children who could make the change to wolves—children whose bloodlines we had lost; whose existence we never suspected. He did it all as a gift to you and you did not so much as acknowledge a single letter!"

One tear escaped to spill down a cheek, and she brushed it away impatiently. "He loved you till the day he died, and he died knowing you had not forgiven him. How could you, Bleidrich? How could you?"

Sebastian had no defence. Saying he had thrown the letters unread onto the fire would just compound his sin. Even without all that he'd heard from Christopher Harris about Nathan's plan, the evidence of his brother's commitment to Sebastian's dreams of restoring the former glory of the pack shone in this house and the children collected here. And thanks to Sebastian's own stubborn pride, Nathan was gone beyond gratitude and reward.

"I am so sorry," he said again. Inadequate, but sincere.

Perhaps Isadora heard the sincerity, for her voice was just sad when she replied. "Sorry does not fix it, Bleidrich."

"You used to call me Bastian," he said. He pulled a handkerchief from a pocket and used it to wipe her eyes, rejoicing when she did not flinch from his touch or slap his presumptuous face.

"No I did not," she retorted. "Nathan used to call you Bastian. I was so overawed by you I could not fit two words together in your presence, and I used to call you nothing at all."

Not as he remembered. She had lit the schoolroom with her presence, enchanting him with her questions and her comments, until he had needed to invent reasons to visit other estates least he take to haunting his underage bride like a lovesick fool.

"I am not your betrothed," she announced. So she had heard that, had she?

"You could be. You should be." She must be. Losing her again would kill him. He would haunt her in earnest then.

She shook her head, though. "Do not be ridiculous, Your Grace. You cannot marry the woman who cuckolded you in the library with the schoolmaster on the night of her betrothal to you. You would be laughed out of Society and I would never be received."

"No-one knows that," Sebastian told her. "No-one who saw you in the library that night remembers a thing, and no-one remembers we were to be betrothed. All anyone knows is that the girl I brought into the house to keep my brother company in the schoolroom married the schoolmaster and moved to another town."

She narrowed her eyes at him. "You tampered with their memories?"

"That very night, to start with. No-one left the library or the ball with any idea that anything had happened that shouldn't. I slept for two days, after. And when I could function again, you and the others had gone, fled that same night, Greville told me. He's the only one who knew what really happened. No. What we thought really happened. Because it didn't, did it Isadora? You created an illusion. If only you had waited to tell us the truth!"

Isadora's eyes widened at that. "But Greville said you banished us. That you would not see us; never wanted to see us again. Nathan told him I was too ill to travel, that I was innocent and you would understand all when you read Nathan's letter, but he insisted they take me with you."

Sebastian was silent for a moment. Greville had been his father's closest friend and Sebastian's most trusted counsellor. Sebastian's last command before he took to his bed was to Greville: *Keep them here. I want to question them. There must be an explanation.* But he woke to find those he loved best in the world had added abandonment to betrayal, and he had been angry ever since. Now, the reversal in his understanding sent his mind reeling, and he took a deep breath as he recovered his balance.

6

Isadora, too, was lost in memories of the past. "Nathan was sure you would send for us, or at least for me, once you read the letter. But at last, when we didn't hear, and when two more letters went unanswered, I married Jemmy." She could not continue to live with two men, neither of them related to her. And where else could she go?

"I never got the letter, Isadora."

She responded to the world of hurt and bewilderment in his eyes, taking both of his hands in hers to comfort him. "Oh Bastian, I am so sorry. Greville never thought I was good enough for you." He had been opposed to her installation at the castle, and argued long and hard against the betrothal.

Sebastian nodded, sadly. "He thought I should marry an earl's daughter, at least. Or his own."

And in the end, he had.

"Ah. Alice. I heard about her death. I am sorry for your loss, Bastian." She was sorry for Sebastian's pain, though Alice Greville had taken her father's part, looking down her pale aristocratic nose at the interloper, saying the courtesy title 'Lady' with near audible quotation marks until Sebastian informed Greville that his daughter was in want of manners.

"Poor Alice," Sebastian said. "I tried to be a good husband; I think I was, at least, a dutiful one, but…"

He tugged Isadora's hands, so that she fell against him, and when he wrapped his arms around her, she hesitantly slid hers around him, thrilling to the hard muscle she could feel beneath her hands.

"The heart of a wolf is a loyal organ, Isadora. I gave mine away when I was twenty. I handed it into the keeping of the woman a ten-year-old would become, and it is yours while I have a breath in my body."

Isadora burrowed her face into Sebastian's chest, afraid to meet his eyes in case it was all a mistake, or one of the dreams that had plagued her lonely nights these ten years.

He continued, his voice low and urgent. "I want you for my wife, for my mate, for my duchess. Marry me, Isadora. I don't care what happened that night. I don't care what was between you, and Nathan, and Harris."

She drew back at that, surprised. "You really do not know? Greville said nothing? You read none of the letters?"

"Only the last; the one that brought me here. I am sorry."

"I was only seconds ahead of you to the library, you numbskull. What you thought you saw was an illusion."

"Yes, I had figured that out. Ten years too late, but I realised when I saw you cast the illusion to protect Mei Ling and the boy. But what was the illusion to cover? That, I don't know."

"Nathan and Jemmy, of course." No understanding in the amber gaze. "You never knew? You didn't realise that Nathan preferred… men?"

She saw him fit the pieces together, caught the flare of anger when he leapt to the wrong conclusion. "His tutor seduced him?"

Isadora snorted, an inelegant and richly contemptuous sound that the elegant Alice would have died rather than make. "Not likely. Jemmy said he was in a position of trust, and Nathan was too young to know his own mind, and Nathan would get over it and find a nice girl, and all sorts of nonsense. Nathan was desperate, because you had said he was ready for university and you were sending him away after the wedding. He… well. Never mind the details.

"But when you asked all those people to the library to see the portrait you had done of me when I was twelve? I couldn't think how to stop you. I could only race ahead of you and try to make them see something they would believe; something that wouldn't get Nathan and Jemmy hanged."

She waited for his anger to flare again, oddly unafraid, confident that he would never hurt her. But he surprised her by ignoring most of the story. "I did not know your gift was so strong, my love," he marvelled.

"Neither did I until I called on it and it answered my need. But I was very sick after. I only know about Greville because Nathan told me. Bastian, you are sleeping in the Masters' Room. Did you not wonder why they shared?"

He gave a wry twist of the mouth. "I had the apostrophe on the other side of the 's', my love. I wondered which of the two was master and slept there. It never occurred to me it was both."

He looked away for a moment, searching for words. "Isadora, are any of the children here yours?"

She heard what he didn't say, and lightly punched his shoulder next to where she had once again nestled her head. "No, you cocklebrain. Jemmy was not interested in me, and—before you ask—neither was Nathan. They had eyes only for one another."

"Then I yet have a chance to win your heart, my dearest love?"

Did the Duke of Denseness really not know? He held himself stiff, as if heaven depended on her answer, and she could not resist. "No, Bastian. I lost it long ago."

"Ah." That was all he said, but Isadora felt his sense of loss as if it were her own, and hurried to reassure him.

"The heart of a wolf is loyal," Isadora reminded him, "and mine was given when I was a lonely girl of ten, a neglected and unwanted daughter being raised by servants. A golden prince rode in on his steed and saved me, and carried me off to be a princess. I loved him then, and through all my great anger, Bastian, I have loved him ever since."

"You love me?" But he gave her no chance to reply, swooping on her lips and greeting her unskilled but enthusiastic response with a joy that quickly flared into something more possessive and thrilling.

She was reeling by the time he reluctantly pulled away. "I had better go, my love, or this will end in your bed, and we are not yet man and wife."

"You want to stop?" She could not believe it. After all the time they had wasted, he wanted to stop?

He was shaking his head 'no' even as he explained. "I have waited ten years, and seven before that. I can wait another week for a special license."

Isadora moved back into his unresisting arms and reached for a handful of hair on either side of his head to pull his lips back down within reach of her own. "You, Your Grace, are a nincompoop. I have waited ten years, and seven before that. And if I have to wait another five minutes, it will be too long."

He had told her once that a wise man, and a wise wolf, knows when to fight, and when to surrender. Her Bastian was very wise, for he argued no more, but simply reached behind him and locked the door.

And the waiting was over.

THE END

My Lost Highland Lass

Interfering relatives, misunderstandings, and mistranslations across a language barrier keep two lovers from finding one another again. The Earl of Chestlewick's daughter comes to London from her beloved Highlands to please her father, planning to avoid the Englishman who married her and abandoned her. The Earl of Medford comes face-to-face with a ghost; a Society lady who bears the face of the Highland lass who saved his life and holds his heart. (Short story)

1

"Is it nearly done, you are, Muire?" Janet asked in Gaelic, half hoping that the answer would never be yes. When Muire had Janet's wild hair tamed into the semblance of an English lady, she would be off to a ball with her stepmother. And which of the three bothered her more—her appearance, the ball, or her father's new young wife—Janet would be hard put to say.

"It will be sooner done if you do not fidget, my lady," Muire replied sharply in English, at the same time giving the lock she held a tug.

Janet subsided, and Muire patted her shoulder. "Peace, my lady. One year you promised his lordship. Less than a year now, and we can go home."

Home. Home in her dear mountains with people she loved and understood: people who needed her. But would they still need her after her long absence? Her cousin Sorcha had been nervous about taking her place, but she would be practiced and experienced in more than a year from now, by the time Janet had made the long trip home to Wester Ross.

"There," Muire said. Janet could see her in the mirror, smiling with satisfaction over the shoulder of an English gentlewoman, her hair rigidly controlled with jewelled pins topped with delicate gold flowers; petals of pearls and amber centres. The hair pins matched the drop earrings and necklace, and complemented the deceptively simply gown in a silk of a dull gold, cut to displayed her white shoulders and her throat all the way to the swell of her breasts. She looked every inch 'Lady Jane', the name these English insisted on calling her.

"Lady Chestlewick should be pleased," Muire said. Lady Chestlewick was unlikely to be pleased with anything short of the demise of her husband's inconvenient Scots encumbrances, but Janet kept that sour thought to herself.

Which was just as well, since the lady herself spoke from the doorway. "I shall be pleased to send word to the coach, Lady Jane, if it suits your convenience for us to leave. We should arrive before the entertainment is quite finished."

Janet rose and turned to face the Countess of Chestlewick, suppressing the fleeting thought that one should never turn one's back on the enemy. Her father's wife was just two years older than herself, and beautiful in the English way, with fair hair piled on her head in pinned curls, one or two teased down beside the diamond-bedecked ears. Diamonds also gleamed from her deep decolletage, diamonds and pale sapphires the precise shade of her eyes and the silk dress that—at least to Janet's healer eyes—imperfectly concealed her condition. Not four months out from the wedding, the Earl of Chestlewick's wife was a bare two months from presenting him with the long-awaited Chestlewick heir.

"I will just hurry to the nursery and say good night to my Katie," Janet said. Growler leapt down from the top of the wardrobe, where the cat had been watching her toilette, and slipped past Lady Chestlewick and out the door. A moment later, his head appeared back in view, his emerald eyes saying, clearly, "Hurry up, Janet."

Lady Chestlewick sighed. "I know better than to argue. One would think a mother would hesitate to disrupt the nursery routine, but my lord indulges you, and so must I. Hurry, then. I do not wish the horses to be kept waiting."

Which meant, Janet supposed, that the coach had already been ordered. She cast a quick glance at the mantel clock. They had yet an hour until the start time of this pernicious ball, though Muire had heard that much of that time would be frittered away in a queue of carriages waiting to drop their passengers at the entrance of whichever mansion held the night's entertainment. "Just a minute or two," Janet replied, soothingly. Growler disappeared again, already on his way to the nursery.

Lady Chestlewick made no reply, but simply sighed again.

2

John Lyndhurst, Earl of Medford, looked over the array of debutantes with a jaundiced eye. How had he let his sister nag him into this? He had fully intended to spend this season as he had the last, attending to business on his estate, riding up to Town for important votes, ignoring the stupidity of the Season as if it did not exist.

He had found the madness hard enough to bear before Scotland. Before her. Since he returned, he had not had the heart for it.

"So. The Cursed Earl has emerged?" He heard the chatter as he passed, circling the ballroom. One of his drinking companions had taken a joking comment made after too much wine and made it into a Society *on-dit* that seemed only to add to the feeding frenzy among the matchmaking mamas. Yes, and the merry widows, who wanted to show they could break the spell that one Scottish witch had cast two autumns ago.

Perhaps his joke had a kernel of truth. Certainly he had not been able to contemplate another woman since he left his Jessie in a remote mountain in the Highlands. He should never have returned to England. He should have brought her with him. He should have sent for her earlier than he did.

He made an impatient gesture to shake off the same dismal round of regrets. He was Medford, and had a duty to the title and the estates he could not abandon. Jessie was too good a woman to set up as a mistress and too wild and Scottish to take as a wife. And by the time he realised what she meant to him and sent messengers, not one could find a trace of Jessie Bowie. Even the remote inn at which they had stayed denied all knowledge of her. It was as if his Scottish witch had never existed, though he yet had the scar from the wound that should have killed him, and that he survived because of her healing Gift.

He was nearly at the bottom of the stair that led down into the ballroom from the entrance hall.

"The Countess of Chestlewick and Lady Jane Amwell," the footman announced. The buzz of conversation stopped, then began again even louder. Rumour had it that the Earl of Chestlewick had sent to Scotland for the daughter of his first scandalous marriage, and Society was agog to see her. Intrigued despite himself, John turned to look.

The two women descending the stairs were individually beautiful, but together they were stunning. The fair goddess had been one of the stars of last year's Season, an accomplishment the young widow crowned when she was married to the reclusive Earl of Chestlewick at his estate just before Christmas. But John gave the countess barely a glance. All of his attention was on the dark-haired lady at her side. Lady Jane Amwell, the earl's Scottish daughter.

She was not Jessie. This woman was thinner; older. Her hair sat neatly in an elegant coiffure, rather than haloing her head in a cloud of frizzy curls. She was no Scottish crofter's lass, but every inch the daughter of an Earl. But she looked enough like his lost love that he started towards her, only to stop when her eyes passed over him without recognition.

She was not Jessie. And he needed a drink. His sister would have to bear him excused, and the debutantes and their mothers would need to hold fire for another day. The Cursed Earl was going home.

3

It was Iain. What was he doing here? Janet would never have come if she'd thought their reunion might take place in public.

Her first week in London, she had sent Muire's husband, Maol-Chaluim or Malcolm as these southerners would have it, to find what he could about Iain Ford—John Ford, the English would say. He had found nothing. She had not yet decided whether to confront the foul betrayer, and now the moment was upon her.

But he looked bewildered. Had she changed so much he did not recognise her? She seized the chance and let her eyes slide over him as if she had never seen him before in her life.

Had he been ill again? He looked thin, almost gaunt, and the laugh lines on his face had been replaced with lines of pain. Her eyes followed him as he turned away and hurried to another exit, almost stumbling in his haste.

"Do you know that man, Lady Jane?" asked the countess.

Janet, unable to speak for fear of tears, forced her face into placid lines and gave her stepmother a smile and a shake of her head. Then friends of the countess hurried up to greet her, and Janet took advantage of their enthusiastic exchange of news to step to back from the group and take a few deep breaths. He had been here. Now he was gone. And if she had had any foolish thought that his betrayal and desertion had killed her love for him, they had been dashed as soon as she saw him.

Somehow, she got through the rest of the evening. The countess had instructed that she was not to dance, and that they would leave after two hours. "Let them be intrigued, Lady Jane. All the better to snare one of them once your Scottish divorce is arranged."

A divorce was probably best, but if her father and his wife thought she would marry again, particularly to another thieving, lying Englishman, they were doomed to disappointment. No. She would stay the year that her father had asked, then leave for home and her clan. And Lady Chestlewick, for one, would be delighted.

Lady Chestlewick looked tired. Sitting opposite her in the carriage, Janet caught the sigh of relief as the countess settled herself on the padded bench. "You need to be careful not to do too much, my lady," she said. "This late in your pregnancy…"

Lady Chestlewick glared. "What are you implying? I have been married but four months, Lady Jane. How dare you suggest that I am approaching my time? I have yet another two months in which Society will expect to see me, and I will not have people suggesting that the child is before its time."

The English were crazy, Janet decided, holding her peace. If the earl and the countess had made a baby before the wedding in the kirk, whose business was it of anyone else? Unless the child had another father? But no. She had seen the couple together. Despite the difference in their ages, they were genuinely in love. Indeed, most of Lady Chestlewick's resentment of Janet herself came from ill-placed jealousy, the lady being resentful of any attention that the earl paid to the daughter of his long-dead first wife.

When the carriage drew up at the Chestlewick townhouse, the earl stood waiting, Janet's retainer Malcolm at his elbow, to hand his wife down. A last-minute late committee meeting at the House of Lords had prevented him from escorting his ladies, but he had hoped to join them.

"You are home early, my dears. I trust nothing is wrong? I was about to follow you to the ball when Malcolm here turned up, and I knew you could not be far behind."

"Nothing is wrong, Chestlewick," his wife assured him, her voice softening as it did for no one else. As he turned to offer her his support up the front steps, she glared over her shoulder at Janet, clearly forbidding her to tell her father her concerns. She followed the couple up the stairs, Malcolm a step behind her. She would say nothing tonight. And perhaps Lady Chestlewick would be more amenable to reason tomorrow.

4

John had done the rounds of the clubs after leaving the ball, finding out what he could about Lord Chestlewick and his daughter. Apparently, as a third son not expected to inherit, the young Matthew Amwell had gone to Scotland, hunting, much as John had done. And, also like John, he had fallen in love with a girl in the Highlands. There, though, their stories diverged. A younger son had the freedom an earl did not. Amwell had made the choice to marry and stayed in the Highlands.

Four years ago, tragedy had struck Amwell's family, taking the Earl of Chestlewick, his father, and then his two elder brothers in quick succession. The third son had come home to take up the title. He was a widower, apparently, and had left a grown daughter behind in the Highlands.

Just the one, the stories all agreed, and certainly only one daughter had answered her father's summons to England after the earl's unexpected marriage. But she might have sisters, might she not? Born, perhaps, on the other side of the blanket, as the expression went? Who knew what a lonely widower might get up to in the long Scottish winters? Surely Lady Jane must be related to his Jessie, and could tell him how to find her?

At three in the afternoon, John sent his card up to Lady Chestlewick and was shown into a comfortable parlour where the countess was taking tea with his sister Margaret Pellingham, and another lady he vaguely recognised. Lady Jane was not present. He suppressed his impatient questions, and endured introductions to her ladyship's friend, Lady Bodwell. He accepted a cup of tea and a seat. He even managed to join the conversation, which was about a proposed trip to see a balloon ascension. Lady Jane did not come.

Thirty minutes was the proper time for an afternoon call. The minutes ticked by, and the lady he wanted to meet remained absent, and the other visitors did not leave. Finally, John asked, "Will your daughter-in-law be joining us, Lady Chestlewick?"

Three pair of eyes, full of speculation, turned to him. "I do not expect her, Lord Medford," the countess replied. "She is in the nursery with her daughter."

A daughter? "But…" John spoke without thinking, but closed his mouth before he insulted the household. Surely the lady was an Amwell? But perhaps she had married a cousin.

Lady Chestlewick made a dismissive gesture. "She also has a husband, my lord. In the Highlands, where they do things differently. Her married surname is impossible for our English tongues. Beenthamisyan, or something of that ilk."

Not his Jessie then. He had not even known he harboured that hope until it was gone, that the elegant woman he had seen last night, every inch suitable to be a countess, might be the woman who had stolen his heart.

"Perhaps you met my daughter when you were in the highlands, Lord Medford?" Damn. He did not want to start yet more rumours, and those about an innocent young woman who would find acceptance in the *ton* hard enough.

"Unlikely, my lady." He kept his tone even. "The Highlands is a big place, and I am sure I would remember the lady if we had met. But I did wonder if we might have acquaintances in common." His thirty minutes was up. He stood to go. "Perhaps I might call again, and hope to meet Lady Jane?" He turned to his sister.

"Margaret, may I escort you home?"

"Mrs Pellingham and I are going shopping after this visit," Lady Bodwell told him. Lady Chestlewick said, "I shall hope to present you to my daughter on another occasion, Lord Medford."

In truth, he realised, as he climbed back into his phaeton, it was as well the lady had not been present. What had he been thinking? That he would ask her if she had a base-born sister? He could not imagine that conversation going well!

5

Janet managed to avoid her mother-in-law for most of the day after an unpleasant interview in the morning that left her shaking. She took Katie to the garden in the centre of the square to spend time with the one person they had so far met in England who seemed disposed to like them. They had met Lady Elizabeth on their first full day in London, when Janet had proposed taking Katie for a walk and her father had given her a resident's key to the garden fence.

Today, as on that first day, they saw the maid first, half asleep in the sun, then Lady Elizabeth on a nearby bench by the fountain in the middle of the garden, reading. Lady Elizabeth looked up when Growler leapt onto the bench and presented his head for her caress.

She smiled down at the cat, and then at Katie. "Hello, little darling," she said. Katie gave her a huge toothless grin, and held out her arms.

"She will crease your dress," Janet warned.

Lady Elizabeth just grinned, and took the baby, bouncing her on her knee until Katie was helpless with laughter and snuggled into the nape of the young lady's neck to sleep.

"Did you enjoy your ball, Lady Janet?" Lady Elizabeth asked. The girl was looking forward to her own first season, but her guardian—'my grumpy uncle', as she called him—had decreed that she would not make her debut until next year. "Which is most unfair, Lady Janet, for I shall be eighteen this year, which is almost old, do you not think?"

Janet managed to satisfy her with descriptions of the gowns, the decorations, and the music, realising as they spoke that she would have enjoyed the event herself if she had felt she belonged, if she had had better company.

"I wish you could have come with me, Lady Elizabeth," she said, sincerely.

"My grumpy uncle went," Lady Elizabeth told her. "Mama says he needs to choose a bride, so he went to the ball, but he told mother at breakfast that he left early, and if she did not like it she could keep her opinions to herself. Which was very rude, was it not? But I am worried, Lady Janet. Mama says she is too delicate to present me, so who will do it if Uncle John refused to take a wife?"

Uncle John? Janet shook off the wild thought. John was a common enough name, and this John was unmarried. Her Iain had a wife. Yes, and a daughter too, though he did not know it.

6

Janet could not think of a good reason to stay away from dinner. The House of Lords was sitting, so the two women ate alone, confining their talk to trivia in front of the servants.

Janet, used to the rambunctious family atmosphere in her grandmother's dining hall, found the near silence oppressive, but she held up her end of the conversation: she had had a pleasant day; she and Katie had played in the garden until rain drove them inside; the dresses ordered from the modiste last week had arrived.

The meal over, Janet would have said a polite good night and taken herself off to prepare for the card party Lady Chestlewick had planned for the evening. But Lady Chestlewick put out a hand to stop her.

"Lady Jane. I have thought much about what you said this morning. Would you mind terribly if we did not go out tonight?"

When Janet had tried to talk to her this morning, Lady Chestlewick had at first denied how advanced her pregnancy was and then become near hysterical with accusations about Janet's supposed hatred for her and the child she carried. "You know that if it is a son, he will supplant you in your father's love," she had declared in close to a screech. Janet had given up trying to talk to her, and had simply found reasons to be somewhere else.

"I am happy not to go out tonight," she said, reluctant to provoke another argument by asking questions. It was a wise decision, particularly now that the rain had become a steady deluge.

"I apologise for what I said this morning," Lady Chestlewick continued. "I do not know what came over me." She blushed and looked at her hands. "I do love your father, Jane. I want you to believe that."

"I know," Janet agreed. "I can see that you love him, and that he loves you. And Lady Chestlewick, I am happy about the baby. I am glad my father will have an heir to his estate and title."

"If it is a boy," Lady Chestlewick said.

It was, and he was her father's son. Janet could feel the child's blood calling to her own. But the English were odd about the Gift, so she said nothing except, "If not, the next one will be, or the one after."

"You are generous, Jane. May I call you Jane? And would you call me Millicent? Your father would be so pleased if you and I were friends."

Janet was willing, and a little guilty about the small part of her that was suspicious of this sudden turnaround. "If you would, my lady—Millicent, I would be happy to have you call me Janet."

"Or even Jessie, as your father does?" Millicent asked.

Jessie (or Seasaidh in Gaelic) was a common enough pet name for Seonaid, which the English translated as Janet, but only Janet's mother and father had used it. Her grandmother had insisted on the formal name, and the clan had followed her lead. Quite why Janet had given her name as Jessie when she introduced herself to the wounded Iain, she did not know, but now she found it hard to hear that name on her father's lips, let alone Millicent's.

"Janet, if you please, Millicent. And if you could persuade Papa to call me Janet, too, I would be grateful."

"If you wish, dear Janet. And I understand. I hate being called Millie, but my first husband would do it!"

Lord Chestlewick's usual worried frown eased when he arrived home to find his wife and daughter were on first-name terms and had spent a pleasant evening together. As he joined them for supper, he exclaimed over how delighted he was that they were becoming friends. Janet was pleased, too.

They had even shared confidences. Millicent had described how the earl's determination not to burden her with a much older husband had led her into desperate measures to convince him they belonged together, and Janet had shared at least some of the story of her meeting with a wounded hunter, their attraction, and their rapid marriage.

Janet's year in England would be much more comfortable if only she and Millicent could be friends.

7

It was pouring with rain when John arrived back in London from three weeks in the country investigating the collapse of a canal on his estate. Rain had been the problem, washing away the footing of the central pillar of a three-arch brick viaduct that took the canal across the river. Fortunately, no one had been hurt, but John had been dragged from London to hear the excuses of the canal builders and the findings of his own men.

He was returning to London determined to find out the link between his neighbour the Earl of Chestlewick and his daughter, and the mysterious Jessie Bowie. His sister might be able to help: she was a close friend of Lady Chestlewick. If necessary, John would ask the earl himself. Asking a man if his daughter had a half-sister might be embarrassing, but continuing to live without Jessie was impossible.

His groom dropped him and his bags at his front door and left to take the weary horse to the livery stable around the corner. John used his own key to let himself in at the door, and piled his wet coat, hat, and muffler on the hall table where they could be collected to be dried. It was not quite dinner time. He could get out of his wet boots and have a nice warming brandy before it was time to change his linen.

A lamp was burning in the library. He looked inside, unnoticed by his niece who was curled in a chair, reading. What a pretty girl she was, and clever, too. When his widowed sister pressed too hard on the topic of his marriage, John sometimes regretted inviting her to make her home with him, but Elizabeth was a pleasure to have in the house.

And dear Margaret would just have to get used to fact that he would chose his own bride in his own time. Just one sight of Lady Janet, who looked so like her, had confirmed it must be Jessie or no one.

He must have made some sound, for Elizabeth looked up. For a moment, she was still lost in whatever story she had been reading, then she launched herself from the chair, her face contorted with rage. "I hate you, Uncle John. How could you do such a thing? Everyone is being so mean to her, and it is all your fault! And Mama will not even let me go and talk to her."

"Elizabeth?" John was bewildered. "Whatever is the matter?"

"As if you do not know! I hate you, and I never wish to speak with you again!" She flung out of the room, and ran upstairs, but not before he had seen the tears streaming down her face.

"Is that you, John?" Margaret came through from the parlour. "What did you say to upset Elizabeth?"

"I have no idea," John told her. "She hates me, she says. Everyone is being mean to someone and it is all my fault. Whatever is she talking about, Margaret?"

"Ah." Margaret paled, and her eyes shifted sideways. Her brother recognised the signs.

"Margaret Pellingham, what have you done?"

Trust Margaret to decide on attack as the best form of defence. "Look to your own behaviour before you criticise mine, John. I am not the one who seduced a gently-born girl and left her with child. And who then told the whole world she was a witch."

John flushed, thinking of Jessie. He had no idea how Margaret knew, but she was right. "I have been hunting for my Jessie these eighteen months, Margaret." He glared, heading off the argument she clearly intended to have. "I will have none other to wife, and so I tell you."

"Jessie? I am talking about Lady Jane Amwell. Why, Lady Chestlewick told me herself. Lady Jane nursed a wounded hunter in the Highlands, and bore his child nine months later. But she did bewitch you. You said so yourself, and I have seen you will not look at another woman, and so I told…"

John stared at her stupidly. "Lady Jane? Lady Jane is Jessie Bowie?"

Suddenly, he turned on his heel and rushed to the hall table, grabbing his damp outer clothing and cramming it on any old how.

"Where are you going, John?"

"To Jessie, of course." Another thought blossomed, spreading warmth through his whole being. "And my daughter." The rest of her discourse fell into place in his mind and he paused for a moment. "And so you told whom, Margaret? All the world, I have no doubt. Without a care for the lady's reputation or mine."

"As to that, neither of you deserve a reputation," Margaret insisted, going once more on the offensive. "That girl insists that she and her lover were wed, but really John, I cannot imagine you lying to get someone into bed. I can only suppose that she fears to tell her father the truth. She would have been better to do so. I live in fear that someone will disclose the story to him, and he will be banging on our door threatening to shoot you."

"Margaret Pellingham, you have been spreading wicked gossip, and I am very displeased with you. I can only hope that Jessie will forgive me. Ponder on this while I am gone. Whether you remain in town or are banished to my most remote estate will depend on whether she can forgive you."

With that parting remark he was gone, out of the door and into the rain.

8

Janet was tired of sniggering, pointed remarks, and snubbing rudeness. She was more than tired of lascivious looks and improper suggestions from men who were certainly no gentlemen, whatever their social class. It had begun more than a fortnight ago, and become so bad that she would not venture out of the house without Muire at her side and Malcolm at her back.

At first, Millicent had laughed it off, told her she was imagining it. And at first Janet interpreted the gleam in Millicent's eye as humour rather than triumph.

But Millicent grew introspective when the gossip and the contempt worsened, when people turned their backs on Janet as she and Millicent approached, when the hum of gossip hushed as they drew near and began again even louder as they walked away.

When a persistent rake tried to drag Janet into the bushes and reacted to being punched in a particularly vulnerable position by calling her Medford's whore, Janet knew that Millicent must have guessed the identity of her hunter and spread the story.

By today, the atmosphere in the parlour had become so strained that Janet had removed herself before tea. She was sitting in the conservatory idling petting Growler while the rain drummed on the roof and ran in sheets down the glass. "I have no idea what to do, Growler," she told him. "I do not wish to cause a breach between Millicent and Papa, but I cannot stay in England."

The cat meowed his agreement, looking up at her with solemn green eyes.

"I will need to explain to Papa why I am breaking my promise. He will be very upset, I think."

"That, my dear Jessie, is something of an understatement." Janet turned, disturbing Growler so that he yowled his displeasure and leapt from her lap. Her father, his face thunderous, was in the entrance. "I will see you in my study, Jessie. I wish to hear from you the truth of these rumours, and I wish to hear from my wife how they came to be spread."

"Papa, remember that Millicent is in a delicate condition," Janet warned him.

Millicent was waiting in the study, pale as death, her eyes bleak. "Phillip," she started.

"I will have your silence, Lady Chestlewick," her husband told her. "We will hear from Jessie first, and then you will explain your part in this terrible situation."

"Phillip, I did not mean…"

"Silence!" Lord Chestlewick turned to Janet. "Be seated, my child. Now. You must not be afraid. Is it true what I heard at the club? That Medford is Katie's father?"

"Yes, Papa. Although I did not know he was the Earl of Medford until we saw him at a ball three weeks ago."

"He is the hunter of whom you spoke? That you found injured, and nursed back to health?"

Janet nodded, and the earl continued, "I thought the man was a Highlander. You did not say so, I realise now. It was just my assumption. But you told me you and this man were wed."

"So we were, Papa. Iain declared us man and wife in the presence of an entire inn full of guests. Do you think I would have given myself to him without at least a promise?"

The earl's eyes narrowed. "He will marry you, if I have aught to say about it. And in an English church."

"No, Papa. I will not have a man who does not want me. He left me. He made no effort to come back to me. Even when we met, he did not come to find me, though he lives right here on the same square."

"He did come," Millicent said. "The very day after the ball, but you were upstairs in the nursery. And his sister says he has spent a small fortune sending agents to the Highlands of Scotland to find the girl he left behind. He has never forgotten her, she says."

Growler leapt into Janet's lap, and she buried her face in his fur, hiding the sudden surge of hope. "That was three weeks ago, and he has not returned."

"He was called out of town," her father explained. "An accident on one of his estates. Had he been here, I dare say he would have pinched this in the bud, Lady Chestlewick, this mischief that you and his sister have made. I am deeply disappointed in you."

Millicent was crying silently, tears streaming down her face. "I am so sorry," she sobbed. "Janet, I am so sorry. I have been sorry almost from the first."

"Of all things I hate, a spiteful malicious gossip is the worst," Lord Chestlewick said heavily, and Lady Chestlewick leapt to her feet and ran crying from the room. Janet started after her, but Lord Chestlewick put a hand on her arm. "Let her go. She needs to think about her sins, Jessie."

"She is in a delicate condition, Papa, and women can have strange moods at such a time, especially if they fear they are unloved."

"How can you say that, Jessie? I… It is not your affair, how I feel about Lady Chestlewick, but I do esteem her greatly. I never thought to marry again, but she… she persuaded me."

"Have you told her of your esteem? You are but five months married, and she bears your heir, yet you spend little time with her. I understand why she was jealous of me."

The earl's frown deepened. "I have my duties at the Lords and to the estates," he said, gruffly.

Janet would have argued more, but at that moment there was a shriek, and several loud thuds as something fell down the stairs. Rushing into the hall, her father on her heels, Janet saw Millicent in a crumpled heap on the landing.

She had no memory of climbing the stairs, just of kneeling beside Millicent feeling for a pulse, checking for a breath.

"Janet?"

Thank God! She was conscious.

"Do not try to move, Millicent. Just tell me what hurts."

"Millicent. Millicent. My darling!" Her father was kneeling on the other side of his wife, holding her hand.

"Phillip? I am so sorry, Phillip. I did not mean to cause such trouble."

"Hush, my love. Let us not worry about that now. Let Janet check where you are hurt."

Below, the door knocker crashed. Once. Twice. Three times. Janet was barely aware, all her attention focused on Millicent. Thankfully, nothing seemed to be broken. She had turned an ankle when she slipped, and sprained a wrist when she tried to catch herself on the way down. But the blow to the abdomen when she landed; that was the biggest concern.

"Jessie! Jessie!" It was Iain, pushing past the butler and shouting as he ran up the stairs. "Jessie, I have to speak with you. I have to explain…"

"Not now, Iain," she said, as the liquids that had cradled her little half-brother gushed from Millicent's womb to soak into the carpet and drip from the landing onto the hall below. She looked up at him, into the steady brown eyes that had won her heart, and then around at the servants who had gathered. "Help me get Lady Chestlewick into bed and send for Muire to assist me. Iain, will you look after Papa, please?"

Millicent's maid turned to Lord Chestlewick, angry-eyed. "You will not let the Scottish witch lay hands on my lady, sir. She might kill the baby!"

Janet stepped back. "You will wish to send for her *accoucheur*, Papa," she said.

"No!" Millicent protested. "I want you, Janet. Please. I feel safe with you."

"You can, my love," the earl said, "she has the Healing Touch, as her mother did. Not witchcraft, but a gift from God."

"I can vouch for that," Iain added. "I would have died in the mountains of Wester Ross. I should have died, but Jessie… Lady Jane, I mean, saved me."

"Janet, please," Millicent begged. "Don't leave me!" And then she whimpered as the first of her contractions came upon her.

"I am here, Millicent," Janet soothed. "Malcolm, help me get her ladyship into bed."

9

John took Lord Chestlewick to the man's own study and poured him a brandy. "You and I need to talk," the earl told him.

"Yes, sir. I came to talk. To you and to Jessie. Believe me, Sir, I have been hunting for her for more than a year, but it seemed she had vanished into thin air! I want to marry her, if she will have me."

"You've married her already, you fool," Chestlewick replied, "or so my Jessie tells me."

John shook his head, but slowly. "Surely I would remember," he said.

In a voice redolent with patience, Chestlewick asked, "Did you by any chance declare Jessie to be your wife in front of witnesses?"

Yes, he had. The first night he was well enough to go downstairs, when someone had asked his relationship to the woman he had been staying with that past three weeks. "Yes. At the inn. I thought to protect her reputation."

"And Jessie was there and did not say you nay?"

Far from it. In fact, it was after that she came to his bed. He smiled at the memory then straightened his lips. He could not say that to her father.

"By Scots' law, Medford, that was your wedding. You took her as your wife in front of witnesses, which is all that is needed. Have you never heard of Gretna."

"But I didn't mean… I do now, of course. You mean we are married? But that is wonderful!"

"As to that, you will have to convince Jessie. Which may not be easy, I warn you. And if she will have you back, you will marry again in an English church, do you hear me?"

Humbly, John agreed. He would do anything. "My lord? Do you think… that is, while we wait… may I see my daughter, my lord?"

10

Millicent did not have any easy time of it, and before they were through Janet had to draw deep on the Gift, but at long last, some thirty-three hours after they had begun, in the early light of a new dawn, the long-awaited heir to the Earl of Chestlewick arrived, screaming his discontent at his early expulsion from his mother's womb.

Millicent, tired and pale, displayed the little Viscount to his proud Papa. "He is so early," she fretted. "Everyone shall know that I… that we…"

"Anticipated our vows? And so we did, my dear Millicent," Lord Chestlewick agreed, with vast satisfaction, Janet's half-brother tucked comfortably under one arm.

"But… the scandal!"

"Will be eclipsed by our daughter's scandal," he replied, as if neither shocking story was of any moment.

Millicent's eyes filled with tears. "Janet, how can you ever forgive me?"

"How can I not forgive the mother of my dear little brother; the woman who makes my father so happy?" Janet bent forward to give Millicent a kiss on the cheek.

"It will be a nine-days' wonder once you have made your peace with your husband," the earl said, "which I hope you will do soon, my dear, for he swears he will not leave until he has spoken with you, and I dare say if you refuse him he shall take root in our parlour."

"He can wait," Janet said, tartly. "I have been working these past two days. I am now going to sleep, and you must as well, Millicent."

11

It was still morning when Janet woke, with the sense that she was being watched. Instantly, she knew he was there. Iain was sitting in a chair by the window watching her sleep, his own face drawn and tired, Growler purring on his knee.

"Traitor," she told the cat. "How did you get into my room, Iain?"

"Your maid, Mary, let me in. I am, after all, your husband, Jessie."

"You have taken some time to remember that."

"I did not know, Jessie. May I explain?"

He was bound and determined to do so, but Janet would have some breakfast while he spoke, and so she told him as she crossed to the bell, wrapping herself in shawl and blushing to be in her nightdress in front of him. Not that he hadn't seen her in much less, and he was thinking the same, the wicked wretch. Just look at the smile on him. She blushed, more at her own memories than at her state of undress.

Soon, though, Muire had brought breakfast, a trolley with food enough for both of them and a large pot of tea with two cups. Once she had left, Iain began his explanation: his lack of knowledge of what claiming her as wife meant, his sense of humble pride that she had chosen him as a lover, the call of his estate and title warring with his desire to stay with her, his realisation that he wanted her for his wife, and finally the dismal reports from the agents he had sent to find his Jessie Bowie.

She sat listening, and Growler, too, though he may just have been hovering to collect the scraps of bacon both of them tossed him from time to time.

"It was as if you had never been, Jessie."

Jessie had to laugh. As if any Highlander would tell an Englishman the whereabouts of one of their own. Though why no one let her know she was being hunted she could not understand. She would ask her grandmother.

Come to think of it, Grandmother had been very insistent that she answered her father's call and come to England.

"Why did you not let me know you were with child, Jessie?" Iain asked.

"And how was I to do that, Iain? You told me your name was Iain… that is, John Ford. But I had no idea where in England you came from, or how to find you."

"Medford," he corrected her. "And it is not my name but my title. And you told me you were Jessie Bowie. Bowie, Jessie?"

"Seònaid nid Buidhe." She spelt it for him. "You would say, Janet daughter of Yellow, which is what the clan called my father when he lived in Wester Ross."

"And Lady Chestlewick said your married name was unpronounceable. Been something."

She laughed again, her heart lighter that it had been these eighteen months. "Bean Thàmhais Iain," she explained. "Janet, wife of Iain son of Thomas."

Iain gave a snort of disgust. "I would have saved myself a lot of worry and trouble, wife of my heart, if I had learned Gaelic in the mountains instead of spending my time letting you practice your English."

She smiled. "Wife of your heart. I like that. And as I recall, Lord Medford, it was not only English that we practiced in the mountains."

Iain leaned forward, his gaze sharpening. Growler made a sound that was very like a snort, and leapt down from the couch beside Iain, where he had been grooming himself after an excellent breakfast. He glared imperiously at Iain until the man rose and opened the door. The cat cast one more look at Janet and stalked out, and John locked it with a click.

"It seems we are alone, Lady Medford," Iain said, crossing the room in a stalk worthy of Growler at his finest. "Shall we practice some more?"

THE END

Magnus and the Christmas Angel

Scarred by years in captivity, Magnus has fought English Society to be accepted as the true Earl of Halwick. Now he faces the hardest battle of all: to win the love of his wife. A night trapped in the snow with an orphaned kitten, gives Callie a Christmas gift: the chance to rediscover first love with the tattooed stranger she married. (Short story)

1

Imperatrix was not in Magnus's chambers. She had not been accidentally shut in the cellars or the attic or any of the dozen unused bedrooms, frozen in a state of readiness for guests who never came. She was not anywhere in the house.

She was not in the stables, or the dairy, or any of the sheds or other outbuildings. The children of the Fenchurch Abbey estate had searched high and low, and brought a score of cats for Callie to inspect, hoping to win the reward.

None of them were Imp.

Callie had questioned all the servants who had cottages near the main house, and none of them had somehow acquired an elegant, imperious, elderly, and very pregnant black cat.

Or not so pregnant now. Imp had gone missing three weeks ago. Somewhere, she had nested and produced her litter. Somewhere— and half an hour ago, Callie had suddenly had an idea about where. They had moved from Blessings more than a year ago, and Imp had birthed two litters since then, her latest at Fenchurch Abbey (in Magnus' dressing room on his cravats). But perhaps she had returned to the place that had been home for most of her life?

Callie shivered, and pulled her shawl further forward over her head. She had run impetuously from the house without first checking the weather, and without telling her maid where she was going, thinking she would not be long.

The clouds looked ominous, but her childhood home was only a brisk walk away; she could be there, retrieve her cat, and be back well before dark. She was not a fool. She wore a rain cape, and it never snowed this far south as early as Christmas Eve. Except, it seemed, this year.

Perhaps it would remain a few stray flakes, melting before they reached the ground, but the sky was black and heavy. She might not make it back to Fenchurch Abbey before the snow began in earnest.

The servants would fret if she stayed at Blessings overnight. Magnus would neither know nor care. He had spent more time in London than at the Abbey since their wedding. Proving his identity so he could take up his title, he said. This was true, but avoiding his unwanted wife was doubtless also on his list of reasons.

His brief impersonal note had said he hoped to be home before Christmas, and she had ordered his rooms prepared: his bed made with fresh sheets, and a fire burned each day to drive the chill and damp from the air. But he had not come. She imagined that London held attractions far greater than the country girl his sense of honour had forced him to marry.

She turned another corner in the path. Here among the trees, the hill between her and Blessings was hidden, but the path was rising and she would soon be at the crest overlooking her destination.

No. She could no longer claim to be a girl. In the years it took him to come home and honour their childhood betrothal, she had left girlhood behind.

Her old nurse would say she was being unfair. Nanny was the only servant to stay with her when she had no money to pay wages after her brother died a year ago and his creditors seized everything moveable.

"His lordship were castaway then seized by savages, Miss Callie, as you well know. He came home as soon as he could escape, and just in time, too."

Yes, and even if she found him much changed—a dour and silent man had replaced the merry boy she had loved her whole life—she was grateful to him for saving her from marriage to his dissolute cousin, who was claiming Magnus's title, his estate and his bride. Wedding Lewis Colbrooke, the putative Earl of Halwick, was a horrifying prospect, but the only path she could see to save her and Nanny from starvation or worse.

Undoubtedly, the gossip about Magnus's reappearance from the dead was still thrilling the *ton*. It was certainly dramatic. He strode into the church and voiced a loud objection to the ceremony currently in progress. "…for she is betrothed to the Earl of Halwick, and I am he!" She had turned, and recognised him immediately, for all that she had not seen him since he was 15, and he was now a man grown, hard, scarred, and grim. In her relief, she had fainted for the first time in her life.

Her thoughts had carried her up the path and out of the woods. From the crest, Blessings should be visible, but the snow was falling more heavily and the path ahead disappeared into gloom. She narrowed her eyes. Was that not a horse? It stood patiently in the swirling snow, while its rider had dismounted and was bending over something on the ground.

Perhaps she could ask for help. She hurried down towards the horse, but her feet slowed as she approached. Surely that was Magnus' horse? And, yes, it was Magnus himself, standing and turning towards her.

In his large hands, something hung limp and lifeless. Something black—an animal. "Imp! You brute, Magnus! What have you done?"

2

Magnus Colbrooke pressed on through the gathering snow, determined to reach home before Christmas. Callie would be expecting him, though whether she wanted him there was another question.

His pulse quickened and his heart sank at the thought of her. Now he had been confirmed as Earl of Halwick, sorted out the mess his affairs had become in his long absence, and made certain his pestilential cousin could no longer trouble him or Callie, he needed to deal with the far less tractable problem of his reluctant wife.

The snow was getting heavier, but taking the short cut through the grounds of Blessings had cut three quarters of an hour from the journey. Even now, he was still closer to Blessings than to Fenchurch Abbey. He would need to push the horse faster if they were to be home before the worst of the storm.

Part of him wanted to turn back to Blessings. Abandoned for more than a year, it would be cold and lifeless, but not as cold and lifeless as his likely welcome from Callie. From the moment she had taken one look at his tattooed face and fainted, he had tried to impose on her as little as possible, keeping his distance. The scars on his face were nothing to the scars on his soul from all he had done to survive during the years of his captivity. He could not bear for her to despise him more than she did already.

A black shape in the snow jerked him from his reverie. Perhaps a rabbit, crawled off to die after being shot by one of the tinkers from the camp close by Blessings. But it was not the right shape for a rabbit.

He could not have articulated why he stopped and dismounted to look more closely. Some vague thought of helping the poor thing, if it still lived. Perhaps he already knew—even from his lofty seat on the horse—what he had found, but his mind chattered on about feral cats and tinkers' cats even as his hands picked up the cold dead body of Callie's beloved Imperatrix.

She was curled around a kitten, as dead as its mother, poor little scrap. What had Imp been thinking, bringing the little one out in this weather?

A gasp behind Magnus told him he was no longer alone; a voice he knew, a scent he would recognise till the day he died even if he never smelled it again, composed of the herbs she strewed among her clothes, the flower oils she used to scent her soap, and something that was indefinably Callie.

He turned to meet blazing blue-green eyes in a white face. "Imp! You brute, Magnus! What have you done?"

"I found her, Callie. She must have been trying to bring the kitten home."

The name slipped out. She had told him that first day, after he interrupted her wedding and proposed himself as replacement groom, that no-one had called her Callie since she was a girl. So he honoured her wish, and called her Caroline. But in his heart, she would always be Callie.

Magnus hurriedly wrapped the cat in his muffler, hoping she hadn't seen the rat bites that scarred her beloved pet. He let her take the cat from him and hug it to her, fighting the urge to put his arms around her as the tears streamed down her cheeks. She would not welcome his comfort, had shrugged it off before. He stood helplessly watching, the little kitten cradled in one hand.

"I am sorry, Caroline," he said, after a while. "I know what she meant to you."

She looked up from weeping into the cat's fur, her eyes still swimming with tears but her face calm. The Callie he had left behind him thirteen years ago showed every emotion on her face. What had happened while he was gone to teach her such control?

"I apologise, Magnus. I know you would not hurt her. Is that her kitten?" She moved Imp to one arm and held out the other hand. Her use of his name set his heart rioting. She did that occasionally; forgot his title and called him by the name she'd used when they were children, and each time his whole being vibrated with the hope that perhaps they could bridge the gap of years to find their old friendship.

"Ah, poor little scrap," she said, echoing his own reaction. Small as her hand was, the kitten filled it.

"Are there more, Halwick?" And just like that, she doused his hope in a bucket of cold titles. He had to wade through his disappointment to comprehend her question.

"More kittens? I have not had time to look, and if there were tracks, the snow has covered them."

"Let us hope they are still safe at Blessings."

She started to walk away, and he turned the horse to follow her. "Why would they be at Blessings? Caroline, we need to get to the Abbey. The storm is getting wilder."

Callie waved a dismissive hand. "You go, if you wish. I am going to Blessings."

Magnus pulled the horse across in front of her, making a barrier. "There is nothing at Blessings. It has been empty for more than a year. Come home, Caroline."

She faced him, white-faced and furious, ready to take on him, his horse, and the whole confounded snow storm. "I am going to Blessings, Magnus. I believe Imp had her babies there, and she died trying to bring them to me. I am not going to let her down."

"It is not safe. There are tinkers camping near. There are no fires, no food. I cannot let you do it." As if he had a hope of stopping her, and so she immediately told him.

"You are bigger than me, Magnus. You can lift me up and carry me to the Abbey, screaming all the way. But as soon as you put me down, I will go to Blessings. If you are so concerned about me, then come and protect me. But I will go to Blessings."

3

Magnus followed her, of course. Callie had known he would. Sometimes she thought the boy she loved was still inside the man who had returned six years late and changed almost beyond recognition. She had always been able to persuade that boy to support her.

"We will go to Blessings, then," he said, "but let me put you up on the horse, Caroline. We need to be under cover before this gets much worse."

He sounded tired, and for a moment she almost turned back. He must have been riding these two days, and she was keeping him from journey's end. But the kittens would not survive if she did not find them, and they were all she had of Imp; a gift from Magnus many years ago, just before his father sent him off to the other side of the world.

But before he lifted her onto the horse, she heard a faint sound. "Magnus, wait. Do you hear that?"

He lifted his chin, his face intent. The tattoos that covered his chin and cheek made his expression hard to read, but after a moment he said, "Yes. Up there."

She looked where he pointed. A large oak tree. A small white kitten clung to a broad branch just above head height, making an occasional attempt to stretch to a hole in the trunk just out of its reach. It had clearly clambered or fallen from the nest, and was too weak to return.

Magnus handed her the reins, and quickly scaled the trunk, returning with the small animal. Callie put its littermate and mother down, and took the living kitten, tucking it inside her bodice, where its tiny cold body could be quickly warmed. It was full-furred, and its eyes were open, but still very young; perhaps the same age as Imp when Magnus rescued her from their tormenting older relatives. And it had not been alone for long, its belly still rounded from its last meal.

Magnus was already back up in the tree, sitting on the kitten's branch and checking in the nest. He met her eyes and shook his head, his own eyes sombre. No more kittens? Or no more living kittens?

"She was taking them home," Callie told him. "She brought them this far, but then the snow came. There is no point in going on to Blessings, now."

"We have no choice, Caroline. We cannot cross the hill in this." Magnus bent to pick up Imp and her baby, and put them inside his coat. He was right. In the brief time it had taken to collect the kitten and check the tree for more, the volume of snow had doubled.

She let him lift her on to the horse, and swing up behind her. The wind was colder this high, less filtered by the low shrubs that bordered the path. He urged the horse into a fast walk, and soon the grey shape of Blessings loomed before them out of the gathering dark.

"I will see to the horse, Caroline," Magnus told her, "while you take the kitten out of the snow."

"Will you leave Imp out here?" she asked. If Imp had been driven from Blessings to save her kittens from rats, as the wounds suggested, Callie did not now want to leave her to them.

"I will bury her and the little one. I don't want…" he trailed off.

"I saw the bites, Magnus." She tried to keep any tartness from her voice. It was kind of him to want to spare her, though she was not the protected child he clearly still thought her.

"Do you wish to… say anything?"

"Prayers, you mean? No, Magnus. I…" she swallowed, as tears thickened her throat, "I will remember her in life, and will not scandalise the rector by demanding a funeral." Her forced laugh sounded more like a sob even to her own ears. "I will see if I can make a fire inside," she said, and fled before she collapsed to cry on Magnus's shoulder.

The house was freezing cold, and empty. Her brother's creditors had stripped it of anything saleable, and broken much else out of sheer spite.

She went straight to the room that had once been the library, the shelves now bare and forlorn. Thank goodness! The marauders had not found the secret room she and Magnus had discovered when they were children. It fitted into an odd corner between a round tower on the original house and the New Wing (built when Charles II was restored to the throne), and no-one but them seemed to know of it. It had become her refuge from her brother and his friends after her father died, and was still stocked for a stay of several days at need.

She bustled about, keeping busy, wondering what was taking Magnus so long. The room was provided with wood to make a fire, and she soon had it started. Next task was a pot of tea—a kettle full of snow melting over the fire and fragrant leaves from the tin of tea she kept on the mantle. The tea was still useable, but unfortunately the food she always kept in her hideaway had long since turned to dust and mould. She tipped it out of the window, container and all.

She collected more snow, using every container she could find, and set it near the fire to melt and warm. Magnus would need a wash when he returned, and they at least had plenty of tea, if nothing more substantial.

If not for her concern about the kitten, she could be pleased to be here again, in the hidden room. Here, the girl she had been and the boy she had loved had talked for hours, studied together, shared hopes and dreams for the future. Perhaps here she could summon the courage to try to find common ground with the man that boy had become, to try to make something real of their marriage.

The kitten revived in the warmth next to her skin, and when Magnus arrived it was in her lap, playing with a ribbon she dangled and occasionally stopping to declare, with a peremptory meow, that a meal might be pleasant at some point in the near future. Poor little thing.

4

It was full dark by the time Magnus had stabled and rubbed down the horse, buried the cat and kitten, and negotiated with the tinkers for food and milk. He had also taken time, in the last of the light, to check the loft over the stable, where evidence of the battle Imp had escaped lay in the scattered bodies of rats. She had made a good account of herself before she set off through the woods in a desperate attempt to bring her babies home.

The snow was sheeting down now, thick and fast. They would be here for the night, and possibly for a day or two. The servants would worry, but he had promised the tinkers a bonus if they delivered the message he had left with them as soon as they could make the trip safely.

He traversed the pitch-black house, heading for the library, in no doubt about where Callie would go to ground.

Tonight, he had seen glimpses of the girl he loved in the still, dignified woman she had become. He had returned from London determined to talk to her, to find out what she wanted for the future. If it were in his power, she would have it, whether to lead her own life apart from him or build the kind of marriage of which they had once dreamed.

He fumbled for the hidden catch that released the bookshelf concealing the door, which opened to light, and heat, and the appealing sight of a pretty woman seated on the floor, her gown pooled about her, playing with a kitten. Her boots were steaming on the hearth next to several jugs and bowls of water, and one stocking foot poked from beneath her skirt, riveting his eyes.

She looked up and smiled, and his heart stuttered. He would give the world to have her look at him like that every time he entered a room.

"Halwick, I have made tea. You will have to have it without milk, I am afraid."

Magnus grinned. "Not so. I have treasures, Caroline. Let me just put these things down and shut the door, and I will show you."

He left the saddlebags in the corner; they would come in handy later. But the basket from the tinkers' camp he put on the floor by Callie, and sat down next to her.

"I have treasures," he repeated. "Goats' milk, enough for the kitten and for our tea too, bread, cheese, and some apples." He handed her each item as he named it: the jug with the milk, the round of bread and wedge of cheese, each wrapped in muslin, and four large apples, undoubtedly filched by the tinkers from Blessings' neglected orchard.

Wide-eyed, she admired his riches. "But how?"

"I saw tinkers in the woods when I rode past earlier. I thought they might be willing to spare a little for us. They offered us a corner of a caravan. The storm will be bad, they said, and the house is inhospitable." The contrast between the tinkers' expectations and the cosy room made him smile. "They have clearly never found our little room, Callie."

Bother. He had called her Callie again, and she was frowning, but not about that apparently, for she said, "I should have stopped to put on my gloves."

"Are you cold, I will…"

"Not for my hands, Magnus. To feed the kitten."

"Ah. Well, as to that…" He stripped off his riding gloves. Stout leather, they would hold milk in as well as they held water out. Callie made short work of turning the thumb and three of the fingers to the inside. He retrieved his belt knife to cut a tiny slit in the tip of the remaining finger, and then folded the tip over to stop leaks while Callie poured some of the milk into the makeshift feeder.

Bent over his hand, she was so close he could have brushed his lips over her hair. Bad idea, Magnus. Or perhaps the best he had had in six months. After all, he had not made much of a job of pretending he did not desire her with every heartbeat, that he wasn't more in love with the dignified woman than he had ever been with the young girl when he was a green lad.

"There. That should be enough to start." Callie sat back and lifted the kitten, cradling it against her breast with one hand while she guided the milk-laden glove to its mouth with the other.

He was a fool. All she cared about was the kitten. But the little mite suddenly realised that milk was trickling into its mouth and began to knead, and purr, and suck, and Callie smiled up at him, her face glowing. "Look at the little angel. Oh Magnus, that is the perfect name for her. Angel. Our Christmas Angel"

"Angel out of Imp, Callie?"

"Well, yes, and why not?" The glove slipped and the kitten complained bitterly. Callie turned her lovely eyes back to her little patient, and coaxed the finger back into its mouth again. To hide his yearning, Magnus got up to wash his hands and slice the bread.

"She must be around three weeks old, Caroline," he said. "Imp has been missing for that long?"

"Yes," Callie confirmed. "We have searched high and low. I her kittens were due, so at first I was not worried."

"She always hides when she has her litter. Not nestled in my cravats, this time." He grinned, to show that he was joking, and after a moment she smiled back.

"I checked there first, Halwick. And then throughout the house, and the stables, and the neighbouring farm." She ran a gentle finger over the kitten's head. It was more than half asleep, its belly round and full. She went on with what sounded like a change of subject. "This morning, Mrs Mallock climbed all the way up to the top floor. One of the new maids found her asleep in the maid's bed. Apparently it was Mrs Mallock's bed when she was a new maid."

"Ah. You thought Imp might have gone back to the days of her first litter."

"She was getting old, Magnus."

"So you came to check the loft over the stable's south wing."

Callie's finger stilled and she looked up from the kitten. "How did you know?"

"You told me in your letters," Magnus said. "Imp always chose that spot to deliver her litters, at the least-used end of the stable, far away from your brother's hunters and their grooms."

5

The hunters on which Callie's brother lavished his attention until he could no longer afford them.

And Magnus remembered her letters? From the day he left, she had written to him. A few lines a day, a letter a week, a bundle of letters posted every month. Trivial stories of a country girl on her ordinary daily round. And he had written back, letters from all down the coast of Africa, then up the other side and into Asia, and across the Pacific. Letters full of exotic stories and drawings of strange and wonderful places.

How boring he must have found her dull and commonplace ramblings.

"I kept writing," she blurted. Letter after letter, at first sent in the hopes the missing ship would finally appear, and later put into the chest where she kept the much read, much cried over letters he had written in return.

"After my ship went down?" Magnus asked, his eyes warm.

Until the evening before her date at the altar to marry Magnus's cousin. That letter, much smudged where she wept on it, and creased where she crushed it in her hands, lay with the others in her chest at the Abbey.

Callie nodded.

"I would like to read them," Magnus said.

Callie shook her head, helplessly. Her domestic ramblings, her outpouring of grief after her father died, her increasing desperation as her brother spiralled down into ruin, stripping the estate to spend his wealth and eventually her dowry on horses, gambling, drink, loose women, and ever more extravagant schemes to rescue their fortunes. Abetted and egged on by his dear friend Lewis Colbrooke, who somehow always seemed to be the winner in any game of chance, and to come unscathed out of any risky venture.

Until the swine won even the deeds to Blessings, and Callie took refuge with Squire Ambrose and his wife.

Magnus took her shake as refusal. "Not if you do not wish me to," he said, the warm eagerness in his eyes turning to disappointment.

"I am afraid you will find them dull," she explained. And far too revealing. She had censored nothing, thinking no-one would ever see them.

"Never dull." The warmth had returned to Magnus's eyes, and his voice slowed to the meditative tones, like rich brandied honey, that always sent a shiver through her. "They were home to me, Callie. I read them over and over again, until they were thin with touching, and they brought me here, to Blessings and to the Abbey; to my own land, and to you. When the ship went down, I had your latest package of letters with me, inside my shirt, and as they hauled me out of the water, all I could think of was that I had a little part of you still with me."

He shook off the mood. "Let us organise a bed for little Angel, and get some sleep."

Callie watched as he quickly and efficiently used an old discarded shirt to line one of the three chamber pots that had found their way here. He placed it on the hearth where it would be warm, but not too hot. Callie wondered if he recognised the shirt. He had been wearing it the day he fought the older boys for two wild kittens, and brought them to her, bloodied but triumphant. Magnus's father had sent him overseas after that, and Callie had washed and kept the shirt.

His next words showed he was traversing the same memories as her. "We did this for Imp and Glad. Do you remember?"

"Yes. We fed them through one of your riding gloves and put them to bed in a… bowl." She blushed a little at discussing such indelicate pottery, and he quirked a grin at her, the tattoos making it seem fierce.

Callie had named the black kitten Imperatrix, Empress, for her regal bearing and clear sense that the world would revolve to her command. The tabby became Gladiator for his combative nature. She had given him to the eldest daughter of a tenant farmer, and Glad lived up to his name, growing to become winner of a thousand barnyard battles and ruler of all the toms for a wide radius around the home farm where he was champion rat catcher and mouser.

"Does Glad still live," Magnus asked, as she settled Angel into the hollow Magnus had warmed by settling the still warm teapot in it for a few moments.

All of a sudden, memories of what she had lost collapsed onto Callie in an avalanche of sorrow. "No. He died last year," she choked out, "and now Imp has gone, and nothing will ever be as it was." Somehow, here in their past refuge, it seemed natural to be in his arms, crying on his shoulder as she had during childhood crises so long ago.

He wrapped his arms around her, rubbed his cheek against her hair, patted her shoulder, and repeated over and over again, "That is right, Callie. Let it out. All will be well. We will make it right, Callie. Let it all out."

It was a long time before she could collect herself, gathering the last shreds of her dignity and pulling away. Except for the night her father died, and the long, long night before the day she was to marry Lewis, she had not cried since she was a girl of twelve, grieving because her dearest friend had been sent to the other side of the earth.

6

Callie cried no more tidily now than she had when they were children. Her eyes were red and swollen, and her nose was running. Another tear gathered in the corner of her eyes as Magnus watched, and spilled down her cheek. He was far gone indeed if he found her desirable even blotched and tear-stained.

"I never cry," she told Magnus, as she took the handkerchief he handed her and blew into it, noisily.

"Then it was clearly time," he said, with a last pat, and took heart when she did not twist away. He dared a little more, and gave her a quick one-armed hug, before saying briskly, "You may have the sofa, and I shall make a pallet on the floor." He handed her one of the other chamber pots. "Here, Caroline. Take it out into the library and leave it there when you are finished."

She blushed, then did as he said, blushing again when she returned to find him in shirt and pantaloons, washing his face and hands. He resisted the urge to put on his coat. She was his wife, after all, and in any other circumstances would, after six months of marriage, have seen him in an even greater state of undress. Except that her reserve, her formality, her obvious fear of his tattooed face (and, did she know it, shoulders and buttocks), had made him keep his distance.

When he returned from the library, she was on the sofa, wrapped in the blanket he had spread for her.

He banked the fire, and blew out the candle, and tucked himself into his own blanket. He had slept on harder floors than this one.

"Sleep well, Magnus." The benediction she had given him years ago, on stolen nights in this room.

"Sleep well, Callie," he returned.

He'd forgotten again, but she did not correct his use of her pet name, just closed her eyes and soon her even breathing said she slept.

He slept too, but woke when the kitten did. Twice, he cradled it inside his shirt while he warmed milk, then whispered nonsense to it as he fed it. Callie must have been even more tired than he was; she did not stir but remained tucked down in her cocoon of blankets.

After the second feed, with little Angel curled in a ball in her chamber pot on the hearth, he checked his timepiece. It was well after eight of the clock, but little light filtered through the window. Even with his nose nearly on the tiny panes of chilly distorted glass, all he could see outside was swirling snow. They would not be going home today.

He fed wood to the fire. He would need to replenish the wood pile, but they could burn some of the broken furniture that littered the outer rooms. Fetching water was of more importance, and best to do that before the tinkers were about. Not that he thought them likely leave their camp in this weather. Nor did he have reason to believe them dishonest, but just in case they decided to take advantage of being cut off from the world to lighten him of the rest of the purse from which he'd paid for the food and milk, he and Callie should stay in their hidden retreat today.

Once he had checked on the wellbeing of the horse, filled every convenient container he could find with snow and set it to melt, used and emptied the chamber pot, and carefully closed the hidden door, he set the kettle to boil. They would break their fast on bread and cheese, and dine on it too, but he had some treats in his saddle bags for a little Christmas cheer.

The toasting forks were where he remembered. He was threading a slice of bread on one when Callie spoke. "I will just attend to… things, and then I will do the toast, Halwick."

"The chamber pot is in the other room, Caroline, where we left it. Come straight back, please. There are tinkers about."

A few minutes later, she returned.

"We used to keep jam…" She fossicked around in the deep cupboard to one side of the little window. "Here! I have it, Halwick. And look," she had the lid off and was exploring the contents with a spoon, "… sugary, but still good. Try some," and she held the spoon in front of his mouth, and he obediently opened and sucked the sweetness.

Having her so close, her face alive and amused, in the hidden sanctuary he'd held in his heart for so long, broke down his defences. He blurted, "You used to call me Magnus. I wish you would again." He waited for her to freeze him with the glare she had perfected, but she simply looked surprised.

"I do call you Magnus."

"Sometimes. You mostly call me Halwick. I keep looking around for my father." He almost accused her of doing it to keep him at a distance, and was glad he had not when she explained, "I have got into the habit, I suppose. At first, I thought to show everyone that I accepted you as the Earl of Halwick, when Lewis kept insisting you were an imposter. You are changed, Magnus. But anyone who knew you would know who you are."

Really? All this time he had thought she was using his title to reject him and she was doing it to support him? "Thank you, Caroline. I appreciate your support."

"You used to call me Callie," she said, her voice sad.

What? But she... "You told me to call you Caroline."

"I did not! When?" Now she glared, but the crease between her brows said hurt rather than anger.

"At St Georges. I said your name and you said you were not called Callie anymore."

Her face cleared. "I did! I said no one called me Callie now. I meant no one knew me well enough to call me Callie, Magnus. And when you started to call me Caroline, I thought you meant to keep me at arms' length." She laughed, the amused gurgle that had lightened his dreams during his years in captivity. "Oh Magnus, how silly. You thought I was calling you by your title to reject you, and I thought the same about you."

A plaintive meow drew her attention to the kitten, which was awake and climbing out of its pot. She scooped it up with one hand and tucked it under her chin. "Good morning, Angel. Are you hungry? Are you hungry, my sweet?"

In the same sing-song tone, so that it took Magnus a moment to realise she was addressing him, and not the kitten, she went on, "But then you stayed away. Even when you were at the Abbey, you saw me only at meals and you were cold and formal. You did not…" she didn't look up from the milk she was pouring into a pot to warm, and even the back of her neck turned bright red, but she did not falter. "You did not claim me as your wife, Magnus. I know you felt obligated to marry me, but I could not help but believe you regretted it."

"No!" Magnus's emphatic rejection startled the kitten and Callie alike, and he moderated his tone. "No, Callie. Never that. If you only knew… But Callie, how could I force myself on you when I am so awfully scarred that you fainted at the mere sight of me?"

Again, her eyes opened wider with surprise.

"I fainted from sheer relief, Magnus. For weeks, months even, I had been trying to find a way to survive without marrying Lewis. He enjoyed it, you know, closing off my options one by one. Lying, bribery, threats; whatever worked to stop anyone from offering me employment or a place to live.

"He told me he could do anything he liked with me, for my only other option was a brothel. He said he could demand that I became his mistress, and I should be grateful he was willing to take me to wife. But I knew he was doing me no favours. As his mistress I would have met other men, and I could, perhaps, have found a way out, even if it were another protector. As his wife, I would belong to him and never be able to escape."

The toast was burning, the bitter smell jerking Marcus from his red rage. "I should have killed him," he said. "I should have let the mob have him, as they wished."

He stripped the toast from the fork, and hurled it into the back of the fire, and was startled when Callie put the replete kitten down and leant forward to put a hand on his shaking arm.

"You saved me, Magnus. I was in despair, and you came."

"Callie, I should have come straight away, as soon as I arrived in England."

"Yes," she said, "You should have."

"I am not the boy who left here, Callie. I am not even the boy who was coming home to you, six years ago. I have seen things, done things to survive that I do not want to ever think about again. You deserve so much better than me. But even I was better than Lewis. When I heard… It was the morning of the wedding, Callie. The trustees for the earldom told me that Lewis was claiming everything. When one of them told me he was even marrying my betrothed—and within the hour—I came immediately. I was so afraid I would be too late."

"You came. You were in time." She had moved even closer, and he yielded at last to the driving urge to take her in his arms. Ah. She fitted as he had always known she would, resting against his chest, her head tucked under his chin, her arms as far around him as she could reach.

"I was in time. And that is why Lewis still lives."

He moved his chin backwards so he could see her. "I thought you were afraid of me, of the tattoos."

She put up a hand and traced the pattern that covered the whole of one side of his face, from jawbone to hairline.

"They are strange, but rather beautiful. Why did they do that to you, Magnus? It seems a strange way to punish someone."

He laughed. "Not a punishment. They mark the face and the body to reward a person, as we hand out medals. Only slaves and children bear no marks."

She traced the marks again. "You must tell me all that happened to you."

Perhaps not all. But more than the bare bones of the story he had given the Committee of Inquiry charged with testing his identity. The shipwreck, the nine months as a castaway, the capture by islanders and the slow steps to win his way free of slavery and into a war band, which he eventually led. And finally, the day an English ship put in for water.

He worked his passage home on HMS Swallow where he occupied a strange position between tattooed savage and Englishman, sailor and civilian, crew member and possible earl. He hid his fierce grin in her hair. Before the shipwreck, his status as an earl's son had protected him from the worst elements on board. As a castaway, he had been the youngest, weakest, and prettiest, at the mercy of the rest. The Swallow crew soon learned that he was a man grown, and a seasoned warrior at that, accustomed to holding his own in a world where promotion was largely on merit.

"The tattoos are not just on my face, Callie." His pulse quickened at the thought of showing her the others, and his smile softened.

A rattle drew their attention to the kitten. It had found the saddle bags, and was batting a loose strap so that it swung and knocked two buckles together.

"Ah, Angel, thank you for the reminder," Magnus said. "Callie, I have a Christmas present for you."

He didn't have to let her go—just lean across and pull the bags towards him, the kitten scampering behind, enjoying the new game. It pounced on the flap he wanted, and he picked it up and handed it to Callie while he pulled out the oilskin wrapped package he wanted.

"Here, Callie. I was going to give this to you for Twelfth Night, but I cannot wait. Merry Christmas."

She turned slightly so she could lean against him and use both hands to unwrap the package, and he kept one arm around her while with his other hand he turned the kitten on its back and tickled its belly with the end of a saddlebag strap.

"Marcus? These are the deeds to Blessings."

"I had them from Lewis just before I put him on a ship for South America. He will not be back, Callie. His schemes and lies and cheating are all public knowledge, and the men he has wronged are baying for his blood."

"And now you own Blessings?"

"You own Blessings. We didn't have time for a proper marriage settlement, and with my identity in doubt... Well, now that I am confirmed as earl, I have corrected that oversight. It is in the package. It just needs your signature. Unless you want changes. I will make any changes you wish, Callie. All I want is for you to be happy."

Callie was crying again, but smiling as well. "You are turning me into a watering pot, Magnus."

He bent to kiss away the tears, and when she turned further towards him to ease that gentle service, he drifted his lips across hers, at first just touching then settling to press and caress. He urged her mouth open with his own, and brushed her tongue with his. Her tentative return thrilled through his body and he sank into the kiss, feeling at last at home, after all these years.

Sharp pinpricks and an anguished yeowl recalled him to himself, and he eased slightly away from Callie to lift an offended Angel from between them.

"Even Christmas Angels should not come between a man and his wife," he told the kitten, sternly. Callie giggled, a happy bubble of a sound that he had heard many times long ago and missed like a lost limb. He bent to kiss her again, holding the kitten out of the way, this time.

"I don't deserve you, Callie," he said again.

"You will just have to make the best of it, Magnus," said his wife. "I waited twelve years for you to come home and another six months for you to come to claim me. I do not intend to ever let anything come between us again. Not distance, not misunderstandings, not even a Christmas Angel."

The Lost Treasure of Lorne

For nearly 300 years, the Normingtons and the Lorimers have feuded, since a love affair ended in a curse that doomed dead Lorimers to haunt their home, the Castle of Lorne.

Now the last Marquis of Lorne, the last of the Lorimers, is one of those ghosts, and the Duke of Kendal, head of the House of Normington, holds the castle.

Kendal doesn't care about the feud or the ghosts. He wants only to find the evidence that will legitimate the son his Lorimer bride bore him before her death, and to convince his stubborn housekeeper to marry him.

But the time allotted to the curse is running out, and his happiness depends on finding the Lost Treasure of Lorne before the 300 years draws to a close.

(Novella)

Prologue

Lorne Castle, Scotland
31st August 1485

The English baroness, cornered at the top of the tallest tower, turned at bay and fixed the Marquis of Lorne with her pale green eyes, her dark hair spilling from her coif and shifting uneasily in the wind.

He laughed his triumph. Now he would complete his revenge. The Normington men had lost him his wife; had forced him to destroy Lorne's greatest treasure. He had hunted down the men, father and son. Only the mother survived. Until today.

Even as he gloated, she leapt up onto the battlement, one step from eternity. Just one step backwards. He grinned. Suicide was a sin, and she as devout as ever trod these stones, telling her beads and praying the hours. Let her call on her saints and her angels for mercy. Only Lorne heard her voice, and he had no mercy in him.

Before he could reach her, she spoke, her voice a low hiss, so cold it froze him in his tracks.

"Hear my judgement, Lionel Lorimer, Fourth Marquis of Lorne.

"By your own actions, you have cursed the house of Lorne. No son of your line will inherit from his father. No daughter will live to raise her own boy child.

"Thus shall it be until the Lorimer blood grows thin. For thrice one hundred years, the gates of Heaven will be barred to the bloodline of this house, and your dead will walk the halls of Castle Lorne, yearning for everlasting rest. Then at the last, Castle Lorne will fall to the enemy, Satan will reap his harvest of souls, and the castle will crumble to dust.

"One chance I give you and only one. If, as the time runs out, the warring houses are united and the last two Lorimers of Lorne find the lost treasure of Lorne, the curse will be over and love will have its reward."

On the final word, Lady Normington took a step backward, and fell silently into the void.

Her body was never found.

Chapter One

Lorne Castle, Scotland
22nd August 1785

His Grace the Duke of Kendal was digging in the moat again. The unusually dry summer had presented an opportunity he could not resist. With the moat almost empty, even the deepest pools came barely to the hem of his kilt. Apart from the boots out of sight under the murky water, the kilt was all he wore.

At not quite forty years of age, the duke was still a fine figure of a man, broad of shoulder, slim of waist, and well-muscled. Even Caitlin Morgan, that stern moralist his housekeeper, paused at the windows of the long gallery to admire the view before she scolded the maids who were doing the same and sent them scurrying back to their tasks. Caitlin stopped for one more glance before resolutely turning away and closing herself in the housekeeper's pantry with her accounts.

The columns of figures were unlikely to drive the sight of a half-naked duke from her mind, but one could try.

Normally, she would do her accounts at night, after the servants— the other servants—had departed for the village. No one but the duke and Caitlin herself would remain in Castle Lorne after dusk. And His Grace's son, John Normington, when he was home from university. Even the duke's valet and butler retreated at nightfall, though only as far as a cottage in the grounds.

The ghosts were a bother, with their moaning and their chatter; which they seemed to understand among themselves, but which stopped somewhere short of intelligible language when they tried to speak to a living being. Any sense was drowned deep under a chaotic racket of hisses, clicks and whines.

Caitlin paid them no mind. She had, after all, spent more than a decade in charge of a rambunctious boy in a nursery, and knew that a little noise never hurt anyone. Besides, for some reason, the ghosts listened to her, and would be quiet if she insisted.

And if she were as much a coward as the rest of them, who would fetch John his supper or keep His Grace company when the male ghosts drove him out of his bedchamber with their carousing?

Not that the duke knew she kept him company. She sat on the secret staircase on one side of the panel that opened into the library while on the other he read a book next to the fire. She frowned down any ghost that thought to disturb him, and in time he would drift off to sleep.

After that one glorious night seven years ago, she did not dare be alone with him. She trusted Kendal, of course. It was herself she did not trust.

Michael held out little hope of finding what he sought in the near-dry moat, and sure enough all he had unearthed so far was cast-off broken furniture and other detritus. The Lorimer family, in their long residence at the castle, had clearly used the moat as a dumping ground for anything too damaged to repair.

Mrs Morgan had told him his quest was in vain, and he was almost certain she was correct. He persisted because of that one slim doubt. No. He would not lie to himself. He persisted because it gave him the opportunity to strip and show his muscles before Caitlin Morgan.

The lovely Caitlin, who hid her beautiful copper hair under dull caps and her glorious curves beneath shapeless gowns.

Loyal Caitlin, who had been with him and John for nineteen years. No. Nearly twenty. John's birthday was this coming October, and he had been only a few days old when his mother died and his great uncle, the last Marquis of Lorne, put the half-Normington newborn out of the castle, exposed on the hillside to die.

Brave Caitlin, who had been thirteen years old when she rescued his son and walked to Edinburgh, daring the soldiers' barracks to find

Lieutenant Normington and break the news to him that he was a father and a widower.

Sweet Caitlin, who had firmly refused that same father's offer of marriage seven years ago, because the deaths of three distant cousins made him a duke-in-waiting. She had continued to refuse it ever since, though he had courted her as best he could and repeated his proposal at noon on the first Sunday of every month.

Not that he would call her 'Caitlin' to her face. Each time he tried, she pokered up and 'Your Graced' him till he surrendered and addressed her once again as 'Mrs Morgan'. She held him off and armoured herself against him with every defensive weapon known to womenkind. But still, she paused in the gallery, half hidden by the drapes, to watch him in his kilt and boots, digging in the moat.

He surveyed the muddy stretch of ground before him. Ten more paces, and he would be back where he started five days ago. In this patch, the puddles were few and only ankle deep, but he would look anyway, raking away the rubbish; poking the steel rod the blacksmith made him every few inches and digging when it hit something hard. He'd found stones and pottery and even a kettle. But never what he sought.

Five weeks ago, as the moat sank lower than even the oldest villager had ever seen, he had set a bounty on every fish and eel, to be caught and released into what was left of the river. Most living occupants of the moat had been rescued more than ten days since, though Michael had found an eel himself the first day of his hunt. Say, rather, the eel found him, latching onto his boot with such determination that forcing it to open its jaws had taken both him and the groundsman who came at his startled yell.

The discovery set off another burst of activity from the village's urchins, but—with no further creatures—they quickly lost interest, and Michael continued his hunt alone.

Five more paces and one last puddle, this one so shallow it barely covered the soles of his boots.

John would be home tonight. He had spent most of his holidays with friends, for which Michael was grateful. He'd be glad to have the lad here for a brief stay before the Cambridge term began again, but friends mattered, especially for a man in John's ambiguous position.

Michael's stabs with the metal rod became more vicious. He would damn the old marquis to hell were it not superfluous. But undoubtedly Satan owned the old man's soul long before he finally choked on the poison of his own hatred and died.

How could he have cursed his own niece's child with the stain of illegitimacy? But Michael knew the answer. Better baseborn than a Normington, or so the last lord of the Lorimers thought. Michael's mouth twisted with bitter amusement. When he had told Caitlin that, she'd said he had it wrong. Lorne did not expect John to live a bastard; he expected John to die on that hillside.

Caitlin, bless her, had confounded Lorne then, and Michael would confound him again. Somewhere in this castle or its grounds, Fiona had hidden the evidence that would prove she and Michael were husband and wife by English law as well as Scottish. So said her last message, smuggled out to Michael before she died. Fiona's father had been in his grave almost as long as his daughter. But somewhere here was the letter he wrote giving his permission for his underage daughter to wed Michael Normington, now—by the grim humour of Fate—the Duke of Kendal, almost the last of his line, and the owner of a castle full of the ghosts of his family's most tenacious enemies.

It wasn't in the moat. A silver casket, Fiona had said, with their marriage lines and letters from both their fathers. Hidden where Lorne would never find it. "The women of my house know," she had said. "Ask my great aunt, Michael. She will show you."

But all of Michael's attempts to see Lady Hannah Lorimer had been thwarted. In the end, he had set himself to bankrupting the Marquis of Lorne inch by inch. Almost a superfluous action. The Lorimers of Lorne were an unfortunate family, much sunk in fortune and number since the fifteenth century.

Lorne was the thirteenth and last Marquis of Lorne, and on his death his title became extinct, his land inherited by the Crown. Large gifts in the right places meant Michael soon owned Lorne Castle. Unfortunately, he was too late. Lady Hannah was six years in her grave, and search as he might, Michael could find no living women of the Lorimers of Lorne, though the dead ones thronged his bed chamber at night, yabbering to him and to one another, an unholy noise that fell frustratingly short of words.

The casket wasn't in the moat. He hadn't thought it would be, but he had to try. His shoulders slumped slightly as he climbed the bank, threw his tools into the waiting wheelbarrow, and picked up his shirt.

He'd sluice himself off at the well in the courtyard before he put the shirt on. It was only courteous to the laundress who would otherwise need to take the mud out of the linen. And if he did not miss his guess, Caitlin Morgan, that stubborn woman, would be at the desk under the window of the housekeeper's room, with a fine view right onto the courtyard.

Chapter Two

There he was again, flaunting his muscles in her direction. Or perhaps he sought the admiration of the maids and the female ghosts. Both groups were watching; the maids finding reasons to pause at windows around the courtyard and the ghosts, flagrant hussies, giggling together in a crowd right where the duke was pouring a bucket of water to stream off his black hair and run in rivulets down his back and chest. They stood so close that his elbow passed through one particularly bold wanton, and she squealed with delight.

Michael could not see or hear the ghosts by daylight; neither the lassies nor the menfolk materialising to chase the laughing girls away, scorching the oblivious duke with black looks that promised a retribution they no longer had the power to deliver.

A rider burst from the dark arch of the gatehouse, bringing his horse to a showy stop inches from the well casing, startling the ghosts into an unnecessary leap to avoid a collision that could no longer have consequences. Caitlin could not have stopped her smile if she wished; she clapped her hands, then closed her books, leaving her room in such haste she abandoned the quill in the ink well.

By the time she emerged into the courtyard, the rider had dismounted to greet the duke, the two of them clasping forearms as they exchanged news of the month since last they met.

Caitlin stopped her precipitous rush, slowing to a walk better suited to the dignity of a duke's housekeeper. Let father and son have a few moments of privacy. She glared at the ghosts, and they slunk a few feet further back, but their movement alerted John to her presence, and he pulled away from the duke and took two long strides to reach her.

"Morgie, darling." For form's sake, she protested as he picked her up, hugged her, and swung her around. She used to greet him in that fashion when he was just a little boy, and he had reversed the tradition when he grew to tower over her.

"You have grown another two inches, Master John. I swear it."

"All the better to lift you, Morgie." He had his father's height, though not yet his breadth, and his father's black hair, close cropped to allow comfort under a gentleman's wig. His eyes were his mother's, blue as a summer sky. Half Lorimer, half Normington, and altogether dear. Caitlin had rescued him and raised him. And if anything in the world could tempt her to throw out caution and common sense and allow the Duke of Kendal to make her his duchess, it would be the right to call this precious boy her son.

But John would be twenty in a week, on the last day of August, and was already making his own place in the world. He did not need her, and Michael would not want her if he knew all.

Caitlin took refuge in her job. "Your room is prepared, and I have ordered a venison pie and carrot pudding for dinner." John's favourites. A stable hand came to take John's stallion, passing heedlessly through the throng of ghosts. Most shifted out of the stable lad's path, but one man in the ruffled collar of a cavalier placed himself four-square in the way as he led the horse to the stables.

The eleventh marquis. The tragedy of the Lorimers and Normingtons had played out in his lifetime, as it had before and since. His daughter had taken her own life after her father murdered her Normington suitor before her eyes.

John and Caitlin both winced when the young groom marched unseeing through the cavalier's chest, then turned to soothe and scold the horse as it danced sideways. The ghost shook his fist in an attempt to further spook the horse, but desisted at their glare.

Chapter Three

"They're here, aren't they?" Michael asked. Before taking ownership of the castle, he had scoffed at the idea that all the dead Lorimers of Lorne still lived here. It was, after all, the eighteenth century; nearly the nineteenth. Superstitions such as ghosts were for the credulous, not for rational English gentlemen.

His incredulity had lasted all of three nights. The first and second night, he had been convinced he was victim of a practical joke. On the third, he had so booby-trapped his bedchamber that the least mouse could not have entered to play ghost. When they appeared anyway, he had been sure he was going insane. Only when he realised that John and Caitlin saw much the same as him did he accept that the Lorne ghosts were real.

The ghosts—most of them—were outraged to have a Normington living in the castle, and managed to make their hostility known without words. The few young women whose love for Normington men had brought them (and usually their sweethearts) to an early death were even more importunate. If only Michael could understand the message they tried so hard to convey.

"The girls were watching you bathe," Caitlin told him, with stiff disapproval, and he felt a spurt of triumph. He was not quite idiot enough to point out she must have been watching herself to see what the ghosts were doing, but his grin must have conveyed the message because she went all Mrs Morgan on him.

"Here is a towel, Your Grace. If you will come inside, Master John, we can do better than well water for your wash, and dinner shall be in an hour. Is that saddle bag all you have?"

She bustled away, sweeping John with her as he explained he had ridden ahead but his curricle would follow within the hour, driven by the manservant who performed all the duties of groom, valet, footman and friend.

Michael followed more slowly, but he had better not delay his own change. In her current mood, Caitlin would order dinner served without him if he were not at table. He might be the duke, but everyone obeyed Caitlin, even his butler. Even the ghosts.

It was just the three of them at dinner. That had been a fight he'd won long ago, when John was old enough to join him for meals. Caitlin would eat with them unless they had guests, and even then she would make up the numbers if they were uneven. It was not hard to make sure they were uneven.

Michael knew what the ton thought about the housekeeper who travelled from house to house with him and ate at his table as if she were family. He refused to forgo the pleasure of keeping her close, even for Caitlin's sake; even when John came home from school with a black eye after fighting for his beloved Morgie's honour.

She was not his mistress, as any servant in any of his houses knew. Why should they act as if they were guilty of something? Even if they once had been. Even if he would be again. In a moment, if Caitlin would allow it.

And if Caitlin wanted to stop the rumours, she could accept his proposal, damn it.

He went down to dinner in a belligerent mood, but the pleasure of sharing his evening with the only two people in the world he counted as family soon dispelled it. John seemed to have spent most of his month away following Viscount Radcliffe, his friend's father, around the man's experimental farm. Stories of mishaps and blunders kept Caitlin and Michael laughing right through dinner, but could not mask John's real enthusiasm for such mysteries as crop rotation and the correct season for manuring.

In another year, he would be apprenticed to Michael's chief steward. The man wanted to retire, and had agreed to stay on until John was ready to take over. Of course, if Michael's hunt was successful, John would one day be the duke, and not just the duke's steward.

The servants were withdrawing now, anxious to quit the castle before darkness fell.

John and Michael brought their port through into the drawing room, and Caitlin excused herself, to return a few minutes later with a tray of tea fixings.

"Are you still hunting for the treasure, Father?" John asked.

Caitlin shared a laughing glance with the lad. "He has been digging in the moat."

"It seemed too good a chance to miss," Michael explained. "No one here has ever seen it so dry."

"It is like this all over the country, Father. It will be a poor harvest, Radcliffe says, and many will lack food and fuel for the winter. He is expecting his poorer tenants to have trouble paying the rent. It's something we should think about, too. You, I mean, sir."

Michael had already spoken to the steward about how they could help, but he encouraged John to share his ideas. What a duke the boy would make.

One by one, various ghosts filtered into the room. Not Fiona. He saw her rarely, and then only in his bed chamber. He had disappointed her, he was sure, in not finding the papers that would establish her son as his heir. Certainly, each time she appeared she seemed more and more distressed.

Her first appearance was the same day as his monthly proposal to Caitlin. He had woken that evening from a deep sleep to find her pacing the room, bristling with indignation to the tips of her nimbus of pale hair. That had been one indication she was a ghost, and not a dream. In life, and when he dreamt of his youthful passion, her hair was a glorious red, bright as flame rather than Caitlin's more subdued copper.

He had assumed she was angry at his courtship, but she nodded vigorously when he pointed out she was seventeen and dead; that he had been a widower for close on twenty years and was far too old for her; that Caitlin would make a wonderful duchess. Whatever her current role in his life, whatever her origins. The surrounding country cast up the Lorimer looks in all sorts of humble families, and he suspected that Caitlin was the offspring of an illicit foray by one of the men of the castle. But bastard and peasant or not, she was every bit fit to be his duchess, and Fiona's vigorous nods made it clear she agreed.

The ghost was upset about something else, and it was to do with his search. Nonetheless, after that he had made his monthly proposal outside of the castle.

Recently, her agitation had spread to the other ghosts. Even the men, who had been hostile since the day he took up residence, now seemed to be asking him for something. And he had no idea what.

Chapter Four

Caitlin spent a restless night ignoring the ghosts, which was becoming more and more difficult. She was in the kitchen and had already stoked the fire to toast a slice of bread when the cook arrived from the village, trailed by several kitchen maids.

"A bad night, was it?" Mrs McTavish asked.

Caitlin nodded, threading a slice of bread onto her toasting fork.

Mrs McTavish shook her head. "I can't say I blame them. Just a week till the young master's birthday and the end of the three hundred years. Sad, that. I can't say but that the villagers will be pleased to see the castle free of its haunting, but it seems tough on the poor ghosties. If only there was someone to help young Master John fulfill the prophecy. Have a care, Mrs Morgan. You'll have the toast in the fire."

Caitlin jerked her head back to the toasting fork, and returned it to the proper distance from the flame. "Just a week?" she repeated.

"Why, yes. Fourteen hundred and eighty-five it was that the Fourth Marquis of Lorne killed his daughter and her lover, and the boy's father and mother for good measure. On the last day of August, so the old stories say, Lady Normington prayed to God for vengeance, and paid with her blood for the justice she sought."

So Mrs McTavish was of the school that held the Normington woman to be a prophesying saint, rather than a cursing witch. And no wonder the ghosts were growing so agitated. But wait. "Master John is a Normington, Mrs McTavish," she pointed out.

"Half Lorimer and living in Castle Lorne. That's been enough to doom someone as a ghost afore now. He is Lorimer enough to find the treasure. But it is too late. Two, the lady said, and he the last Lorimer of Lorne."

This time, the toast caught alight before she noticed. It was not just what Mrs McTavish had said that distracted her, but the reaction of the ghosts. Crowding into the kitchen, row on row, even standing in the fireplace itself, they were cheering and clapping.

John counted as a Lorimer? She had known that two were required, but—like the cook—she had believed only one remained. The King's heralds had hunted down all branches of the Lorimer family tree and so had the Duke of Kendal, looking for one surviving twig, and coming up empty. They were wrong.

Caitlin knew, as no other living person knew, that Caitlin Morag Lorimer, granddaughter of the last marquis, had not died in an unseasonable storm twenty years ago, the night after his niece died; the night that he carried his great nephew out into the howling rain to perish on the hillside.

Her grandfather scowled at her from behind the celebrating wraiths. She resisted the urge to make a rude face at him, contenting herself with a broad smile. The devil could have the sour old buzzard—him and the others of his line who had sacrificed a daughter to the continuing feud. But perhaps she and John could save the others.

She made a fresh piece of toast, buttered it and spread it with preserve, kept up a conversation with Mrs McTavish, wrote the shopping list that one of the senior maids would take to the village shop, and sent the parlour and chamber maids off about their work in the rest of the castle, all the while thinking about where the treasure might be, and how to tell John who she really was.

Michael—that is—the duke had searched high and low and discovered nothing. And he, at least, knew he was looking for a silver casket, but Caitlin had no idea what the lost treasure might be, or how large a space would be needed to hide it.

She took John's breakfast up to him herself, over the protests of the valet. No time like the present to begin. He was awake, and sitting up in bed, but pulled his blankets up to cover his bare shoulders. "Morgie!"

Caitlin ignored his embarrassment. "Put on your robe, Master John, and come sit at the table. There is something I need to tell you." She glared at the ghosts who emerged from the floor, having followed her from the kitchen. "And you lot can all take yourselves off. You are not invited to this conversation." She put the trolley with the breakfast next to the table by the window, and turned to see him still sitting clutching his covers.

She raised her eyebrows and he heaved a sigh. "Very well. But wait in the hall while I put some clothes on. Please, Morgie. I'm not five any more."

Michael found her standing in the hall outside John's door, tapping one foot while she waited, ignoring the few spectres who had braved her wrath to wait with her. He looked barbarously regal in a scarlet banyan embroidered with gold and silver dragons over a silk shirt with a lace jabot. Under it, he wore his usual kilt, with knee-high silk stocking and soft indoor slippers. Would this be the last time he looked at her with such warmth? She could not expect—she would not ask John to keep her identity secret.

He sounded amused when he said, "Will the young scoundrel not let you in, Mrs Morgan? Shall I wake him for you?" He did not wait for a reply, but opened the door, and John choked his startled protest when he realised it was his father, and not Caitlin, that had burst in.

A murmur of voices, a long silence, then Michael opened the door. John was now wearing a banyan too, a garish concoction in purple with large orange flowers that bore no resemblance to anything found in nature. Beneath, she could see his breeches and stockings, and the frill of his shirt. Undoubtedly, he had not thought it proper to entertain her without dressing.

"May I join you for breakfast, Mrs Morgan?" Michael asked. "Or is this a private meeting?"

Caitlin hesitated a bare fraction of a moment. He would find out anyway, and there was no time to waste. And his search had made him as familiar with the castle as anyone on earth. Perhaps he could help. "Very well. Fetch yourself a chair and a cup for your coffee."

The three organised themselves: Caitlin pouring coffee for Michael and his son, and tea for herself; Michael and John filling three plates with bread rolls, bacon, eggs, sardines in mustard sauce, slices of cold pie, mashed potatoes and spreads from the trolley. All the time, Caitlin thought about what she needed to say.

"This is nice," John said, "but what did you need to tell me, Morgie, that could not be said in front of the servants?"

Caitlin avoided Michael's eyes. "Mrs McTavish has just informed me that the three hundred years of the curse ends on John's birthday."

Both men froze, and then put their forks back on their plates, the better to consider this news.

"This is good, is it not?" Michael ventured. "Isn't the haunting meant to end with the three centuries?"

"But what of the ghosts?" John demanded.

"I suppose they will get their rest at last," Michael said, soothingly, "and not before time, poor souls."

"That's not what the legend says!" John turned to Caitlin. "Is it, Morgie? Don't they all go to hell?"

"No!" Michael turned to Caitlin too. "That's not fair, is it? All of them?"

"That was Lady Normington's curse. Or her prophecy." It occurred to Caitlin that she'd not heard the story from any of the castle servants. Indeed, until this morning, none of them had mentioned the Normington-Lorimer feud or the curse. "What do you know of the legend, John?"

"Very little," John admitted. "Just what I've overheard. The servants won't speak of it to me."

Caitlin queried Michael with her eyebrows, and he shook his head. "Me neither. I am still the Normington interloper."

"The feud, then. Do you know how the feud began?"

Michael shook his head. "I did not even know there was a feud until Fiona said her uncle would never consent to our marriage because I was a Normington. Perhaps my cousins knew, but mine was not the senior line, Caitlin, as you know. What have you heard?

Caitlin took a deep breath. She would tell the story as she had heard it from her great aunt; as it had been passed down through the generations.

Chapter Five

"It began more than three hundred years ago. The Marquis of Lorne was a great power in the land, which at that time was split between those who supported the King of Scotland, and those who—secretly or not so secretly—wished his eldest son to rule. Lorne played both sides. His youngest daughter, Lady Morag Lorimer, attended the Queen at Stirling Castle, and his sons served the king in Edinburgh.

"It was in Edinburgh, on a visit to her brothers, that Lady Morag met the handsome son of an visiting English nobleman, Stephen Normington. Black of hair, he was, with pale green eyes that saw into her soul. And he was just as bewitched by her, that Scottish lass with her rich red hair and her milky skin that felt like silk to his touch. For touch her he did, and more, and they plighted troth to one another so she was his true wife, or so the young couple thought."

Michael gave a shiver at that, and Caitlin paused in the telling, knowing he was remembering himself and another girl with the Lorimer hair and complexion.

"They thought?" John prompted. "Were they not married then, by Scottish law?"

"They were not, for Lady Morag was not free to make her vows. Her father had promised her to another man, and had signed the betrothal papers, though the girl was unaware. And when she told her father she was wed, he flew into a rage. He and his sons carried her off to Castle Lorne. What happened there, no one knows. Her mother took her part, or so it is whispered, but mother and daughter disappeared and were never seen again.

"Young Normington came hunting for his wife, and was struck down. His father followed, searching for his son, and Lorne had him and all his soldiers killed, though in the fight his own sons also died.

"Finally, Lady Normington appeared at the gates, begging for the bodies of her dead so they could be given Christian burial. Lovely, she was, with the colouring of her son. And barely in her thirties, for she had been only fifteen when she bore Stephen, and he just sixteen when he stole the heart of Morag of Lorne."

"Poor children," Michael commented. He and Fiona had been older by a single year when they met in Edinburgh.

Caitlin continued. "Had Lorne gone mad in his pride and grief, or was this the moment that pushed him over the edge? He let her into the castle and promised to meet her request, and all the time he plotted her undoing. He had what was left of the bodies retrieved from the carrion pit into which they had been thrown, and let her tend them with her own hands, wrap them in strong linen with many sweet unguents and herbs, and lay them in oaken caskets.

"All that night the coffins lay in state in the castle chapel while the lady knelt between them, praying. And in the morning, Lorne gave her his ultimatum. Wed him and give him two sons and a daughter to replace those the Normingtons had taken, or he would throw the bodies back into the carrion pit and take her for his leman, will she nil she."

It was Caitlin's turn to shiver. It was this part of the story that had won the marquis the name Lorne of the Black Heart. Lady Normington must have known a moment of deep despair, but she had returned a soft reply.

"Give me this day to mourn my husband and my son, and I shall fast and pray for wisdom to respond to your request," she asked Lorne. Lorne was conscious of the castle folk at his back. They had not interfered with his revenge, and were as fierce as him at fighting the English. They'd not protect the woman from his rape nor prevent him from desecrating the corpses. But he had heard their whispers of admiration—at her courage in venturing into the castle, her loyalty to those she loved, the devout way that she prayed. He would find no support for stopping her at her prayer.

"This one day, then," he growled, and he went off to his meal, leaving a strong guard on the chapel door.

"He was outside drilling with his men when one of the guard came running to say that Lady Normington was no longer in the chapel. The guard had not moved. No one had passed them coming or going. But the chapel was empty of any living person."

Caitlin let the silence drag for a moment. Two moments. Three. Until John asked the question for which the storytelling ladies of Lorimer always waited. "Where had she gone? How did she escape?"

"No one knows how Lady Normington escaped. As to where she went, Lorne had his men search the castle, high and low. It was on high they found her, in the tallest tower, and as Lorne came closer, she climbed higher still until she was on the tallest battlement and he knew that he had her at his mercy."

"But when he cornered her, she spoke doom on the house of Lorimer, and stepped to her death."

Caitlin deepened her voice as Aunt Brenwyn always had, repeating the final words of the lost lady:

"By your own actions, you have cursed the house of Lorne. No son of your line will inherit from his father. No daughter will live to raise her own boy child.

"Thus shall it be until the Lorimer blood grows thin. For thrice one hundred years, the gates of Heaven will be barred to the bloodline of this house, and your dead will walk the halls of Castle Lorne, yearning for everlasting rest. Then at the last, Castle Lorne will fall to the enemy, Satan will reap his harvest of souls, and the castle will crumble to dust.

"One chance I give you and only one. If, as the time runs out, the warring houses are united and the last two Lorimers of Lorne find the lost treasure of Lorne, the curse will be over and love will have its reward."

"And ever since, the Lorimers have waned and the Normingtons have waxed, until today, nearly at the end of three hundred years, the curse has almost played to its end."

That was the easy bit. As she looked from father to son and back, she prepared herself for questions. Now she would need to tell them what she had hidden for twenty years. But Michael's first question wasn't what she expected.

"That's it? That's why Lord Lorne refused to acknowledge my marriage to Fiona? He'd make the two of us miserable and his own great nephew a bastard for something that happened three hundred years ago?"

"Not just that," Caitlin assured him. "The story has played out again and again. Six other times a Lorimer lass and a Normington lad have fallen in love, thought to unite the warring houses, and died. Eight times in all, counting Lady Morag and Lady Fiona.

"Each time prompted more enmity between the two families. Every conflict between Scotland and England; every conflict between King and would-be King since the nations became one, the Lorimers have been on one side and the Normingtons on the other. And the Normingtons have ever chosen the winning side."

Caitlin tipped her head as she considered Michael. Three hundred years ago, the Normingtons had held a barony and a reasonable competence. Now, the head of the house was a duke, and a wealthy one. And he was impatient to hear the rest of her story. "Go on," he said.

"The Lord Lorne who denied you and Fiona had a sister who was one of the lost daughters, and her Normington lover killed Lorne's cousin, who was his uncle's heir, before dying himself. Lorne also blamed the Normingtons for the loss of his own heir. The man died at the Battle of St Cast when your predecessor's son failed to bring up his troops in support."

Michael shook his head. "I knew nothing of this. Perhaps my parents did not know. They were estranged from the elder line of my house. Certainly, they did not say. Why punish us for the deeds of others?"

"It is said among the Lorimers that the tale and the ghosts drive the men of the house mad. And on this one point, the feud with the Normingtons, the former marquis would not be moved from his hatred. Even to the point of infanticide."

Michael turned his green gaze on his son. "John unites the warring houses," he noted.

Caitlin nodded. Fiona had said the same thing when she handed her baby to Caitlin nearly twenty years ago. "Love him, Katy, darling. Guard him well. When he is old enough, send him to his father. John unites the two warring houses, and will end the curse."

But Lord Lorne had taken the baby from his cradle and sent him out to die in the September rains, and Caitlin had stolen out of the castle to keep faith with Fiona.

"He is the first," she told Michael. "Others before you and Fiona were wed, at least by Scottish law, but none lived long enough to bear a child."

"But it is too late, isn't it," John argued. "You've checked, Father, and the last Lorimer of Lorne died years ago. Even if I count as a Lorimer, I am only one." He looked at Caitlin, frowning. "The last two Lorimers, you said, Morgie. I am only one."

Caitlin took a deep breath. This was the moment she had been dreading. Now she must tell Michael that she had lied to him for twenty years. She looked away. She did not want to see the affection drain from his eyes.

Michael spoke into the silence. "Caitlin, what are you afraid to tell us?"

Chapter Six

If Caitlin had not been sitting, she would have fallen. She had been pale when Michael saw her in the hallway, and as she told the barbarous tale, all colour had drained from her face, leaving in high relief the few pale freckles remaining from the constellations that had starred her face when she first arrived in Edinburgh.

What worried Michael most was that his prickly bossy housekeeper would not meet his eyes, but sat looking down into her lap, where her clasped hands showed white knuckles.

Michael covered her hands with one of his. "Caitlin? You know we will not think the less of you whatever you tell us."

She did not push his comforting hand away, which he counted a gain, but nor did she look at him. Instead, she answered John. "You are not the only Lorimer of Lorne, John. My real name is Caitlin Morag Lorimer. You and I are the last two, and we are the only ones who can find the lost treasure and save the ghosts of Castle Lorne."

Now she looked at Michael, and Michael looked back, blankly. His enemy's granddaughter. When Lorne's men had come several days after Caitlin's arrival eighteen years ago, he thought they were after the baby. He had hidden John out of town, in a friend's remote hunting lodge, leaving Caitlin to care for him, telling no one. And just as well, too, for Lorne's men had searched everywhere and questioned everyone. John shook off the memory of a dark room and pain, and a closer brush with death than he cared to consider. In the end, his friends had found him, and Lorne had never found John; had clearly decided the baby had never reached Edinburgh.

And all along the man had also been looking for his granddaughter whom Michael had been hiding unknowing.

Dimly, through the deluge of emotions, he noted Caitlin's pallor had increased, which he had not thought possible, and her lovely eyes held quiet despair. Thank God his shock had frozen him, for the first reaction was past and he had not pulled away. He gave her hands a squeeze.

"We owe you even more than I realised, Caitlin. You gave up everything to save John." His voice was steady, if his heart wasn't. His enemy's granddaughter! The heir killed had been her father, and Michael himself had killed her uncle when escaping from the man's torture.

The colour returned then, flooding her face, and she blinked away tears. "Not as much as you might think." She smiled at John; a weak effort, but still a smile. "And I had John."

And me, Michael wanted to say, but he held his tongue while John hugged her and then scolded her, "Why did you not tell us, Morgie? Did you think we would stop loving you?" A grin spread across his face as the knowledge sunk in. "You are my cousin. Father, Morgie is my cousin." He hugged her again.

"I was your mother's cousin, John, and am yours," Caitlin confirmed.

John had more questions; was near bursting with them. But he stopped with his mouth open to speak; focusing into the empty space over Caitlin's shoulder, closing his mouth and turning his head as if tracking movement across the room.

"They're here?" Michael asked. "The ghosts?"

"Some of them," Caitlin agreed. "Reminding us that time is running out. We must solve the mystery by the end of this month. John's birthday."

"Right." John crossed the room to fetch his writing desk and Caitlin cleared a space for it on the table. "Let's make a plan. Father, you have been searching whenever we came to Castle Lorne for the past three years. Where should we start?"

"Not for the lost treasure," Michael objected. "I was looking for—something else."

John stopped in the act of trimming his quill. "I always assumed—but if not the lost treasure, what?"

"Proof of my marriage, John. You know you are my legitimate heir here in Scotland, and in any case will have anything of mine that is not entailed. But that b–" Michael caught back the word; the old bastard was Caitlin's grandfather and he'd not upset her for the world. "The Marquis of Lorne destroyed the records and bribed or threatened the witnesses so the marriage would not stand in England. He claimed that Fiona's father—your grandfather—had not given consent. She was of age in Scotland, but not in England, and without his consent the marriage did not stand. Not in England."

"But my grandfather could give him the lie."

"If he'd lived to see what Lorne did. Your grandfather was sick with consumption, John, but when Fiona wrote to him to tell him we had wed, he sent a letter giving his blessing. She wanted to see him one more time, and with peace between the families, as we thought, there seemed no harm in it. I got leave to take her to Glennevis, but he was dying then and I had only four days. Fiona wanted to stay. I should never have left her, John."

"You could not have known," Caitlin assured him. "And she does not blame you, Michael."

"Is that my mother, Morgie? The one patting Father's shoulder?"

Caitlin nodded. Michael managed not to flinch away from the touch he could not perceive. "Waving goodbye to me as I left her at Glennevis was the last time I saw her alive, my sweet Fiona. I guessed, of course, that Lorne had her. As soon as I heard Stuart Lorimer was dead, I rode for Glennevis, but I was too late. Lorne had taken her, but he kept her hidden and while I hunted for her, someone burnt down the little kirk where we'd made our vows."

"But if the records are gone, and the letter is gone..." John protested.

Michael didn't wait for him to finish. "Fiona had the proof. She smuggled a letter out to me, from one of the places Lorne kept her while he was wiping out all record of our marriage. She told me to come to Castle Lorne once it was safe, and to ask one of the women of the family to show me the secret hiding place that only the women knew."

"Caitlin is a woman of the family," John pointed out, but Caitlin was shaking her head.

"I left Castle Lorne when I was thirteen. I never learned the secret."

"It is somewhere here," Michael insisted. "A silver casket containing our marriage lines and letters from both our fathers. She said to ask her great aunt, but I could not come near, and the old lady was six years in her grave by the time Lorne died."

"But this is good," Caitlin told him. "We now know that there is a secret hiding place. Surely the lost treasure will be there, too. If– when we find it, we will have both the proof that John is your rightful heir, and the salvation of the ghosts."

John disagreed. "If it were that simple, one of the ghosts would have solved it while they were alive. But Father, your search is a help, nonetheless. Where have you looked?"

"Everywhere. I don't think there's an inch of wall or floor I have not covered, and the grounds, too. I've found nothing. Hidden places, but they've been empty. Forgotten rooms, even, but none with what I sought."

"We'll start again, then," Caitlin decided. "We can't give up, Michael. And with three of us hunting, perhaps we'll be lucky this time. Will you help?" The last was clearly addressed to the ghosts. But the hope in her eyes faded to disappointment.

"Did they refuse?" Michael asked.

"They disappeared." Caitlin stamped one foot. "Surely one of them knows? Do they not realise that in this we are all on the same side?

Chapter Seven

Three days later, they had retraced Michael's treasure-seeking steps throughout the castle, from the attics of the tallest towers to the lowest of the storerooms in the cellars.

John's birthday dawned, and still they had not found the treasure. They were covering some of the same ground now, banging on walls in the hopes of hearing something hollow; trying to turn the flourishes in carved wall panels and frames in case one of them unlocked a hidden door.

"What time of day did Lady Normington pronounce her curse?" John asked, as he circled the dining hall for the third time that day, so intent on his search that he walked right through the watching ghosts.

Caitlin didn't know, and so she told him.

The approaching doom did not seem to make the ghosts more agitated than usual. Indeed, the usual group of women carried on mysterious tasks in the corner, as they had for weeks, often joined by one or more other ghosts.

The duke's man of business arrived, and monopolised his master's attention for most of the afternoon and into the evening, but Caitlin and John carried on the hunt until they had to change for dinner and pretend to the man of business, who was staying overnight, that nothing was amiss.

Once he was safely off to bed, the three of them met in Michael's private sitting room to wait for midnight, and in ones and twos the ghosts seeped through the walls to join them.

"Do you suppose the servants are mistaken about the date?" John asked as the clock chimed eleven times. Several of the ghosts looked up from whatever they were doing and shook their heads.

"Then about the consequence," Michael suggested. "You will stay in the castle, and not all be forfeit to the devil."

But that suggestion set off not just a flurry of shakes but a mournful wailing.

"But if the curse is true and the date is true…" Caitlin said, as the ghosts crowded around her nodding, "then we have less than an hour to find the answer." The ghosts seemed to lose interest, wandering off again to their corners.

"I can't think of anywhere we have not looked," Michael grieved. "Fiona." He stood in front of the ghost of his young wife, so that she had to look up at him. "Fiona, I want to help. Can't you tell us how to find the treasure? And the casket with the marriage lines? Please, Fiona."

But Fiona slid her eyes away from him and circled around him to join the others in the corner.

They watched the hands of the clock shift with glacial speed towards midnight, and still the ghosts remained, even after the thirty-first of August became the first of September. Caitlin had no idea what she expected. Anything from a silent disappearance to Satan himself arriving in clouds of fire and sweeping her relatives into the maw of hell. For nothing to happen at all was almost a letdown, relieved though she was.

"Is the clock slow, perhaps?" John suggested, and they waited another interminable half hour.

"We might as well go to bed," Caitlin said at last. "Either the legend is wrong or the date is."

"The date!" Michael stopped short, halfway across the room to the door. "It isn't the thirty-first of August."

"No," John agreed. "It is after midnight."

"That's not what I mean. The Calendar Act. The Calendar Act, Caitlin."

"Michael, you are not making sense."

Michael caught her hands and almost danced her across the room.

"No, listen. We have another eleven days. You're too young to realise, it isn't three hundred years for almost a fortnight."

Caitlin glanced at John who looked as mystified as she. "You will need to explain."

"The dates changed. The whole calendar changed. They took eleven days out to bring us in line with the rest of Europe. I was born under the Julian calendar and had my first birthday under the Gregorian. It became a joke in my family that I was always in a hurry to get places, and even had my birthday early. My mother used to wish me a happy natal day on the date I was born, and another eleven days later on the actual anniversary."

The ghosts did not look enlightened. But then the confusion of sound went both ways, and Michael's explanation was far too complex to put into simple mime. Unless… Caitlin stepped in front of Fiona, attracting her attention, and held up both hands, then folded down one finger after another, and both thumbs, tipping her head to one side and raising her brows in question. She did it a second time, and a third.

Other ghosts gathered to watch, and John came to repeat the gestures at her side, and then Michael, who added a pantomime at the end in which he pointed to the ghosts, and swished his fisted hands from side to side, as if scrubbing something out.

The ghosts vanished. Every single one, disappearing in a moment.

"What did I do?" Michael wondered out loud, but before he could finish the sentence, they were back, watching him expectantly, glowering or smiling according to their nature.

"Do it again," Caitlin said, and led the two men, holding up both of her hands to start the sequence, all the way through to the scrubbing motion. The ghosts were gone as she finished the motion, then back in before she had time to blink, the bolder ones grinning broadly, and clapping.

"We have ten days before they vanish," Michael concluded.

"Ten days," John said, "to find Lorne's treasure."

Chapter Eight

They went off to bed, but Caitlin's mind kept worrying at the problem. After trying and failing to find a comfortable position in which she could sleep, she gave up and lit her candle so she could make some notes on new places to search. Not that she could think of any.

But the candle light showed seven of the ghost girls, including Fiona, standing in a row and staring at her. "I am trying," Caitlin told them.

Seven girls, all in a row. All with the distinctive Lorimer features. The lost ladies of Lorne? The tale said there should be eight—eight times a Lorimer lass and a Normington lad had loved, and eight times the lass had died, with Morag the first and Fiona the last.

But wait. What were they doing? All of them were suddenly busy, quills or needles or brushes in hand, writing or sewing or drawing. A few moments of feverish concentration and then an orchestrated pause with all eyes on Caitlin. Again the activity followed by the stare. And again.

It was a clue. It had to be a clue. But what did it mean?

"There is no point in further searching," Caitlin announced in the morning.

John frowned. "You are giving up?

Michael looked up from sprinkling salt on his porridge. "Not our Caitlin." He gave her a warm smile. "What do you suggest?"

"Not me. The lost ladies." Caitlin told them about the early morning game of ghostly charades.

"But what on earth could they mean? The secret is in writing or...? Oh." John trailed off as he put it all together.

Michael had figured it out too. "You think the ladies have left instruction in what they've written, drawn or sewn?"

"We need to check the library." John was already standing, pushing away his plate.

Caitlin gestured for him to sit down. "We need to check the library, the attics, every desk and chest, and every wall. But first, we need a plan and you might as well eat your breakfast while we discuss it, John, for we have a busy few days.

After breakfast, Michael ordered trestle tables set up down the centre of the banquet hall, and sent servants to fetch every image that might have been created here at Lorne or by a lady of Lorne. Every watercolour, oil painting, line drawing, embroidered image, or tapestry. Framed or unframed. In the attic or the cellars or anywhere between. On walls, cushions or chair covers. Large, medium-sized or small. The servants spread out and began returning with their finds.

Michael had had no idea that there were so many, and no notion where to start, but Caitlin ordered the smaller ones laid out on the nearest table, as many as it could hold, then began at one end, pointing to an image while staring into empty space, her eyebrows raised in question.

Ah. Clever girl. She was asking the ghosts whether this piece of artwork had significance.

As Michael watched, John nodded and stepped forward to remove the painting, while Caitlin moved on to the next. Several of the local servants could also see the ghosts, it seemed, for they stepped forward too, to follow Caitlin down the row removing the images that the ghosts refused but leaving a good number on the table.

Or was it the other way around? No, because Caitlin said to the butler, "You might as will have the discards rehung, Masterson. I am sorry for all the work."

"Not at all, madam. We are happy to help," Masterson said, bowing slightly before he ordered some men to the work.

What a woman. When even a very proper English butler recognised her quality, surely a duke could only take heed. Of course, he knew now why she did not wish to marry him. The Normingtons were responsible for the deaths of her father, so many of her kin. He himself had killed her uncle and stolen her heritage. But, he had also loved her and protected her and if he could not change the past he could at least put her back in the position to which her birth entitled her. By all holy things, he would have this out with her once they'd found the treasure and saved the ghosts, for if he could not have Caitlin Mo– Caitlin Lorimer as his wife, he'd have none.

By the end of the day, they had the images sorted and had begun on the words. Books, diaries, letters, recipe folders. Every single piece of paper with any kind of handwriting on it from any corner of the castle, which had seemed large yesterday and now appeared vast.

A third long row of trestle tables had been set up to contain them all, but Caitlin's heart sank at sight; stacks, piles, and drifts of paper covered with writing, some double and even triple crossed.

Michael put an arm around her and squeezed her shoulder. "We'll start in the morning, Caitlin."

John was back at the other tables, walking slowly along, looking at the images that Caitlin had roughly organised by topic. "I don't understand. I can't see the connection."

"Not all of them will be clues, John. Some will just be what they appear. Women are taught to paint flowers and baby animals and the activities of daily life." But Caitlin had hoped for something obvious: a map, a drawing of a secret door in a wall, a set of instructions.

Tomorrow. Tomorrow they would tackle the books and letters. The ghosts had been so insistent. What they wanted must be here somewhere.

Chapter Nine

With no idea what they were looking for, the going was slow even after they roped into the task any halfway literate servant, but three days later the document mountain was significantly reduced, and Caitlin had half-filled a notebook of her own with snippets of text, observations, and ideas.

She was reading some of the quotes to the two men, as they took their dinner on a cleared corner of the table.

"This one was in a diary from one hundred years ago. '*Today, my aunt showed me the hidden way to where the two stand guard. I must practice to be able to open it by myself, in case I am the one to meet the key.*'

"And this from another. '*My daughter will turn twenty next week. Is she old enough to understand that the secret must never be shared with a Lorimer man, for the curse drives them mad?*'

"This was in the margin of a recipe book, beside a recipe for ox-foot soup. *Four to open, Two to guard, Two to unlock, and One to waken.*' I wrote it down because of 'two stand guard', which is also in this poem.

> "*I practice the four to open the door*
> *The way is hard to where two stand guard*
> *When the time is through, then come the two*
> *The first to be last, redressing the past.*"

Michael tore his bread roll apart with a focused savagery. "'I practice the four'. The four what? Why could they not be plain?"

"Because the curse drives the Lorimer men mad," John suggested. "They needed to hide the secret from the Lorimer men."

Caitlin waved her notes. "I have more. The same messages in different words over and over. Four to open, two to guard, two to unlock, and one to be woken, or sometimes one to be last. A few of them say three to find the way. But mostly, they agree on two."

John waved his bread roll at Caitlin. "The two to unlock are you and me, but what is it that we awaken?"

"Only one of us, if we are the unlockers and if the unlockers are the same as the awakeners," Caitlin corrected. "The note says 'one to awaken'."

"I practice the four." Michael repeated. "I practice the four. Do the paintings help? What comes in groups of four?"

"The ghosts in the corners," John said, dryly, then sat forward in his chair and repeated it. "The ghosts in the corners, Caitlin. What are they doing?"

Caitlin grasped the candelabra that had been lighting her way as she read and led the way to the nearest corner, where one ghost sat, her hands busy, while three others watched. They looked up as the live people approached, and then the seated ghost bent back over her hands and the other three lowered themselves into ghostly chairs that suddenly appeared to receive them, and began to feverishly copy her movements.

"They are sewing," Michael decided.

"Yes, but what?" John was leaning so close to the original ghostly sewer that her shoulder disappeared into his upper arm. She ignored him, continuing to move her hands above the shadowy cloth in her embroidery hoop as if plying her needle, but try as they might, they could see neither the needle nor the image she was creating.

Of the other three, one appeared to be mending, one working on a large tapestry frame, and one sewing down the long seam of a pieced shirt, her movements so evocative they could almost see the needle flying in and out.

"I think I have it." Caitlin spun around to stride down the length of the hall to the next corner, the men hurrying to catch up. "If I am right, these ghosts will be writing or drawing or painting."

They were. Five of them this time, all women. One painted with an invisible brush on a miniature canvas held in her hand, another worked at an easel. A third held a sketch book open on her knee, while the fourth bent over a lap desk and a fifth over a ghostly table, both writing feverishly.

Caitlin led the way again, saying, "Stillroom work." It was. Three ghosts this time: one tying bundles of herbs; one stirring something in a pot over a fire they could not see; one carefully measuring ingredients from an array of bottles, jars, and pouches that appeared in her hands as she took them up and disappeared as she put them back down again.

"So what is the fourth?" Michael asked on their way back down the other long side of the hall, "and how do you know?"

Caitlin diverted to the tables where the paintings and drawings lay in stacks. "I've seen the four groups of activity, but did not make the connection." She began sorting, searching, and soon had four paintings that were clearly done by the same artist and meant as a group. Same size, same illustrative techniques, and the same woman in each. In the first, she sat mending a shirt. In the second, she was painting, four small canvases lined up before her. The third showed her in the still room, pouring liquid from a small kettle through a funnel into a bottle. And in the fourth, she smoothed a cloth over the forehead of a child who was tucked up in bed.

Caitlin found another frame, this one with four miniature paintings side by side. Four sets of hands. The first holding a needle, the second a quill pen, the third a still room jar, and the fourth a spoon.

Getting the idea, John and Michael began re-sorting the paintings. "The fourth is sick-room care," Michael announced.

"Any type of care, maybe," John corrected. "If these are part of it." He had found several images of women carrying babies, and presenting food or drink to children or men.

"Let's see what the ghosts have to tell us." Caitlin approached the fourth corner, where one ghostly lady walked to and fro with a sleeping baby cradled on her shoulder, and another kept watch by a sickbed. The third ghost in this corner was Fiona, who approached Michael and offered him a goblet. "Care," he murmured, putting out his hands for the goblet, which evaporated at his touch. Fiona smiled, and turned to John, presenting him with a ghostly plate of his favourite oat biscuits.

The hall was full of ghosts now, the sounds of their celebration so loud that it almost breached whatever barrier prevented the living from understanding the dead.

And if that were not enough to confirm the ghosts believed they had solved the puzzle, Caitlin's grandfather clinched it. He scowled at her from behind the celebrating wraiths and she grinned back. He might be happy to roast in hell for the sake of his feud, but clearly the remaining ghosts saw her and John as their salvation.

Chapter Ten

"I practice the four," Caitlin repeated. She had collected the tools and materials she needed, and visited each corner of the room: mending one of John's shirts, writing a letter to Michael which she folded and sealed, making the simplest oatmeal water by soaking oatmeal groats in water then boiling it over a spirit stove for five minutes and adding cinnamon and sugar, and replacing the dressing and bandage on Michael's long scratch. But nothing had happened.

"I practice the four," John agreed. "But where, Caitlin?"

"Anywhere in the castle if we're to do as the ghosts do," Michael said. "They set up wherever we are."

"What is my mother doing?" John asked, and Caitlin and Michael turned to watch Fiona as she crossed from them to the door, and then returned, beckoned, and went back to the door. They followed, escorted by most of the ghosts, along the hall and down the stair to the entrance floor, then out a door at the rear and through the cluster of new service rooms built onto the old keep, into one of the medieval towers, and through that to the large room that the Lornes had most recently used as a ballroom, but that had once been the chapel.

"Here?" Caitlin asked. "I am to do the four tasks here?"

Michael suggested leaving it till morning, but Caitlin and John declared themselves too anxious and excited to sleep and soon Caitlin was repeating the four tasks again, one in each corner.

A mended *fichu*. A carefully inked drawing of the Rose window at the narrow end of the room, where the sanctuary would once have been. A tisane of ginger and lemon verbena.

On her way to the fourth corner, she passed Michael, who had subsided on one of the chairs that lined that wall, and was sitting with his head back and his eyes shut, his face in repose showing the effects of too little sleep and too much worry.

Caitlin stopped to lay a hand on his arm. "We will solve the riddle, Michael. If this isn't the answer, we'll keep trying."

He cracked one lid then the other, and put his hand across to enfold hers. "If it can be done, you will do it. I trust you, Lady Caitlin Lorimer. But one more try for tonight, and then bed, my dear. You are working yourself to a shadow."

Yes, Michael needed to sleep, and John too. As for Caitlin, she longed for her bed with a deep fervency. "One more try," she agreed. "Then bed for us all, and a good breakfast before we begin again."

Michael patted her hand and the quirk in the corner of his lips spread to become a full smile. "Dearest Caitlin; still looking after us all."

"Father? Morgie?" John's hushed tone warned them before they looked away from one another and saw the transformation. The room was no longer a slightly shabby ballroom, neglected and in disrepair. Instead, the ancient chapel lay all around them, statues and tapestries restored to the walls, memorials to Lorimer ancestors lining both sides, the altar rising high under the rose window, and before it the one sight that drew their eyes, casting all the rest into insignificance.

A fog occupied the centre of the chapel crossing; a dark cloud that churned and shifted, but neither drifted from its place nor dissipated. The waiting ghosts watched, but none approached the fog.

Michael leapt to his feet. "The casket!"

It was there, exactly as Fiona had described, placed close to the point where the fog almost reached the nave of the chapel. Michael was on it in a moment, and his eyes lit with triumph as he opened it and then the papers it held.

"But what is inside the fog?" John demanded to know, and strode towards it, only to be hurled back. He picked himself up before Michael and Fiona could reach him. "I'm not hurt. But rushing it clearly isn't going to work."

"Two to unlock," Fiona reminded him, and took his hand. Cautiously, they tried the fog again, and each time it repelled them, though with less force than the first.

"Try by the back, where Fiona left the casket," Michael advised.

Carefully, still holding hands, counting backwards from three, John and Fiona reached out a hand each to touch the fog, and it disappeared, disclosing a bier, draped in black. On either side, a woman knelt, her head bowed, the palms of her upraised hands facing the bier and her counterpart. The bier was occupied. A young woman, clearly pregnant, her arms crossed on her chest above the swelling of her belly, her red hair spread loose across the pillow on which her head lay.

Caitlin broke the silence. "Not ghosts." Not shades of white and transparent. Not floating at a slight angle to reality, but solidly on the flagstones.

John's voice was awed. "Look at their clothes. Is it Lady Morag, do you think? The one that started it all?"

"Yes." Michael's voice was as hushed as her own. "And the two mothers. Lady Lorne and Lady Normington."

At the sound of their names, the two ladies opened their eyes and looked around.

"It is the three, Fionella," the lady with the pale green eyes said, "just as you foresaw."

"One of mine, Anne," said the lady whose eyes were the same blue as Caitlin's and John's, "one of yours, and one from both of us."

"And not before time," Lady Normington added. "The three hundred years is almost done."

"Tell us how to break the curse," Caitlin begged.

"Not a curse," Lady Normington corrected. "A blessing, to hold our granddaughter safe until the feud was over."

"For three hundred years?" John, as if drawn by a rope, was taking one slow step after another towards the bier.

"To Morag, it has been but a single night's sleep; a night in which my friend and I watched over her in a space outside of time," Lady Lorne explained.

The green eyes twinkled. "They think us witches, Fionella." Lady Normington smiled at Michael. "You do not believe in such things, I know. And that is not the case at all. My friend has the sight, a gift of dreams. In her dreams she saw the destruction of both our houses within a score of years if Lord Lorne concluded his revenge in the way he intended. He had already, in his pride, tried to kill his daughter and unborn grandchild, though Morag had been his greatest treasure since her first breath. They were saved only because Fionella hid them from him.

"So we prayed together, Fionella and I, and we were given a space of a night for the three of us, and the space of three hundred years for our families to find a path to peace or destroy one another."

Lady Lorne took up the tale. "My friend spoke her prophesy so the whole castle could hear, giving the Lornes a reason not to wipe the Normingtons from the face of the earth, and then returned to me in the chapel. We taught my sister and my niece how to find the chapel if they needed it, by doing the tasks that men never consider important."

"And then we waited," Lady Normington said, as if removing a chapel from a castle and the bier into a space entirely outside of time was a matter of little difficulty.

"We waited for you, child." Lady Lorne's eyes settled on John. "You are the one who can awaken."

"What must I do?" John asked. He was standing over the bier now, looking down on the face of Lady Morag Lorimer, whose love for a Normington had been the catalyst for all of this.

"You know what to do," Lady Normington told him. Her voice sounded further away. She was fading, becoming transparent. Lady Lorne, too.

John had no eyes for them. He was leaning over Lady Morag, bending to place his lips on hers. And as he kissed her, a great ringing sounded, and the world seemed to quake, though nothing moved.

Lady Normington and Lady Lorne winked out of existence. The ghosts, too. Without a farewell or any fanfare, they were just gone. But not Lady Morag, whose eyes were fluttering open.

❦ ❦ ❦

Chapter Eleven

The messenger left before noon, carrying the precious missive that would summon Michael's lawyers to begin the steps to have John recognised as his legitimate son and rightful heir. He'd completed one of his tasks for the day. Now for the other, more important, mission.

Last night, Caitlin had been totally absorbed in Lady Morag and her plight, waking three hundred years after falling asleep, with everyone she knew long dead. But this morning, the young lady was showing a marked preference for John's company, and John could not take his eyes off Morag.

"I dreamed," she explained at breakfast. "I saw each of the doomed couples, and the death of each Marquis of Lorne, and I knew that the years were passing, though it seemed to me a single long night." She looked at John from under her lashes. "I saw you, too, sir." And she blushed, which set John blushing.

They were off outside somewhere, the butler said. Lord Kellering was showing Lady Morag around the estate. Michael had to smile at the courtesy title John should have held since Michael himself ascended to the dukedom. Fiona would be pleased, and old Lorne must be screaming with rage in the hottest fires of hell. Which reminded him of his purpose.

"And Lady Lorne? Did she go with the two young people?"

He and Caitlin had argued about that over breakfast, and Michael won. As the last living grandchild of the Marquis of Lorne, Caitlin was his heir. Michael had always intended to petition the

Crown to recognise John, heir through his mother, but Caitlin's was the better claim. Marchioness of Lorne, and her first son Marquis to re-establish the house her grandfather and his predecessors had destroyed.

They'd have to prove her birth and her identity, and the House of Lords, Society, and the papers would buzz with arguments for and against for months, but Michael had made a start by instructing his household staff that his former housekeeper was now to be treated with all the dignity due her rank.

"Her ladyship is up on the tower, I believe, Your Grace," the butler said.

Michael didn't have to ask which tower; she had returned to where it all began: the feud, the curse, the centuries' long wait for Michael and Fiona and the son they made.

He hurried up the long curved stair, and she was there, looking down over the battlements, her hair escaping from the cap she wore to blow in the wind that always caressed the upper reaches of the castle, no matter how still the day was below.

He thought he had been quiet, but she spoke without looking around. "Will they make a match of it, do you think?"

"John and Morag?" Yes. There they were, just coming up the hill from the village, her arm through his, he curved as if to hear her better or to protect her, or both. "John wants to ride for the bishop and a special licence," he replied. "He says he'll have none else to wife, and he wants her child born within wedlock."

"He'd make another man's child his heir? Your heir?"

Michael shrugged. "If it is a boy. The ladies said a granddaughter, but John says it does not matter. Morag's lover is three hundred years dead, and a Normington besides. I would rather speak of your heir, Lady Lorne? Will he be half Normington?"

Caitlin turned her head to face him, doubt and hope warring in her eyes.

"Are all the barriers gone, my lass?" He managed to sound calm, but he would beg if he had to. "Or do you hate me for what my family has done to yours."

Shock flared. "No!" She clasped his hands, squeezing as if force would convince him of her earnestness. "No." More quietly this time. "Both families have paid an awful price for the Lorne obsession. But I do not blame you. How could I? I lo– I love John." She turned away again, hiding her blush. Michael relinquished one hand but held on to the other.

"Only John?"

"I thought you would hate me. My grandfather condemned your wife, lied about your marriage, tried to kill your son."

Michael gave her back her own words. "I do not blame you. How could I? I love you."

"You are fond of me, I know. And grateful to me."

"I love you," Michael repeated. "Caitlin, I want you for my wife, my duchess, and if you will not have me, I shall remain single all my life. I love you."

"You love Fiona," Caitlin reminded him.

"I loved Fiona with all the passion of a young man's heart, and when she died I thought I would never love again. But then a young girl grew up in my household. I fell in love with her courage, her loyalty, her intelligence, and her beauty. Bit by bit I discovered that a man grown can love more deeply than a stripling, and that one does not need to throw out the old love to make room for the new. My heart shaped itself to hold you, Caitlin. Don't force it to live empty."

She wouldn't look at him, kept her head turned away. But she did not pull away her hand. Indeed, she pressed his before she spoke. "I wanted to hate you. For being a Normington. For taking Fiona from me. But I had nowhere else to take John, nowhere he would be safe. And from the moment I met you, I knew I could trust you to protect us. Oh Michael, I have loved you since I was a girl."

She was in his arms then, her lips reaching for his, and he lost himself in the warmth and the taste of her. He had no idea how long it was until he withdrew his head enough to speak, dazed but determined. He could not forget that their last kiss, seven years ago, had taken them into bed together, but ended with her withdrawing beneath the protective shield of her housekeeper caps and aprons. "Is that a 'yes', Lady Lorne? Will you do me the honour of being my duchess? Shall I fetch two special licences from the bishop?"

Her answer glowed in her eyes, but she said it anyway. "Three questions, Your Grace, but a single answer. Yes."

In the corner of his vision, Michael sensed a shimmer, and he and Caitlin turned in time to see the ghosts of Lady Lorne and Lady Normington, hovering above the battlements, smiling a blessing on them.

Their voices sounded distant, but without the interference that had made the castle ghosts impossible to understand.

"It is finished, my dear friend," said one.

"Yes," said the other. "Now we can go home."

And with that, they were no more.

Jude Knight would like your help

Book reviews help readers to find books and authors to find readers. I work in a day job until my books earn enough to allow me to write full-time. If you like my writing, please help free me to do more of it, by telling your friends about me and asking your local library to stock copies of my book.

Also, please consider writing a review for *Lost in the Tale*, even a couple of sentences telling people what you liked (or didn't like) about it. *Reviews* can be posted on Goodreads and on most eretailers' websites. For links to this book on those sites, see the *Lost in the Tale* page on my website: http://judeknightauthor.com/books/lost-in-the-tale/

News and special offers

Subscribe to Jude's newsletter for information about publication dates, advance information about release dates and special price periods as well as exclusive, subscriber-only special offers and an exclusive short story each issue. Jude sends a newsletter up to six times a year. New subscribers receive a link to a page full of free short stories and novellas to download as ebooks.

You will find a subscription link at http://judeknightauthor.com

Acknowledgements

Thank you to all those who helped me put this book together: to the five prize winners who ordered the stories, to my dear friends and colleagues, especially Mari Christie, Sherry Ewing and Carol Roddy, who read early versions of some of the stories and helped me work out plot hiccups, to my wonderful team of beta readers, especially Sue McGaw and (for *The Lost Treasure of Lorne*) Kathryn Reeves, whose comments and questions helped shape the final versions of the stories, and to my husband who, as always, kept me fed and dragged me from my computer occasionally to remind me that the sun still shone.

Bluestocking Belles

The Belles are eight very different writers united by a love of history and a history of writing about love. From sweet to steamy, from light-hearted fun to dark tortured tales full of angst, from

London ballrooms to country cottages to the sultan's seraglio, one or more of the Belle's will have a tale to suit your tastes and mood.

The Belle's blog, *The Teatime Tattler*, publishes at least twice weekly, with exclusive news, interviews, and scandals set somewhere in the fictional history of one of our correspondents.

The Belles have committed to publishing at least one box set per year. Proceeds from some of the Belles' joint projects go to the Malala Fund, to support education for young bluestockings around the world.

Find the Bluestocking Belles online:
www.BluestockingBelles.net/
Friend us on Facebook:
www.facebook.com/BellesinBlue
Follow us on Twitter:
@BellesInBlue

Malala Fund

The Bluestocking Belles have chosen the Malala Fund as the charity we support and to which we donate communal royalties. Periodically, we take on projects intended to directly support this cause, which exemplifies our personal values and intentions: the right of girls and women to do whatever they choose with their lives.

For more information about the Malala Fund and the founder, Malala Yousafzai, winner of the 2014 Nobel Peace Prize, go to www.Malala.org.

Holly and Hopeful Hearts

When the Duchess of Haverford sends out invitations to a holiday house party and a Twelfth Night ball, those who respond know Her Grace intends to raise money for her favourite cause and promote whatever matches she can.

Eight assorted heroes and heroines set out with their pocketbooks firmly clasped and hearts in protective custody. Or are they?

Jude has two stories in *Holly and Hopeful Hearts*: *A Suitable Husband*, and *The Bluestocking and the Barbarian*. They are also being published as stand-alone stories.

Never Too Late

Eight authors and eight different takes on four dramatic elements selected by our readers—an older heroine, a wise man, a Bible and a compromising situation that *isn't*.

Set in a variety of locations around the world over eight centuries, welcome to the romance of the Bluestocking Belles 2017 Holiday Anthology. It's Never Too Late to find love.

Jude's story in *Never Too Late* is set in Victorian New Zealand, at the time of the Tarawera volcanic eruption. *Forged in Fire* is the story of two English people far from home.

Burned in their youth, neither Tad nor Lottie expected to feel the fires of love. The years have soothed the pain, and each has built a comfortable, if not fully satisfying, life, on paths that intersect and then diverge again.

But then the inferno of a volcanic eruption sears away the lies of the past and frees them to forge a future together.

Jude's published books

Candle's Christmas Chair

When Viscount Avery comes to see the best invalid chair maker in the southwest of England he does not expect to find Minerva Bradshaw, the woman who rejected him three years earlier. Or did she? Older and wiser, he wonders if there is more to the story.

For three years, Min Bradshaw has remembered the handsome guardsman who courted her for her fortune. She didn't expect him in her workshop, and she certainly doesn't intend to let him fool her again. Even if he is handsomer and more charming than ever.

Gingerbread Bride: A novella in the Golden Redepenning series

Lieutenant Rick Redepenning has been saving his admiral's intrepid daughter from danger since their formative years, but today, he faces the gravest of threats—the damage she might do to his heart. How can he convince her to see him as a suitor, not just a childhood friend?

Travelling with her father's fleet has left Mary Pritchard ill-prepared for London Society, and prey to the machinations of false friends. When she strikes out on her own to find a more suitable locale to take up her solitary spinsterhood, she finds adventure, trouble, and her girlhood hero, riding once more to her rescue.

Gingerbread Bride is a novella in *The Golden Redepennings* series and was first published in the Bluestocking Belles' box set *Marriage, Mistletoe, and Mayhem.*

Farewell to Kindness: **Book 1 of** *The Golden Redepennings*

Hidden from the earl who hunts them, Anne and her sisters have been accepted into the heart of a tiny rural village. Until another earl comes visiting.

Rede lives to avenge the deaths of his wife and children. After three long years of searching, he is closing in on the ruthless villains who gave the orders, and he does not hope to survive the final encounter. Until he meets Anne.

As their inconvenient attraction grows, a series of near fatal attacks draws them together and drives them apart. When their desperate enemies combine forces, Anne and Rede must trust one another to survive.

A Raging Madness: **Book 2 of** *The Golden Redepennings*

Ella survived an abusive and philandering husband, in-laws who hate her, and public scorn. But she's not sure she will survive love. It is too late to guard her heart from the man forced to pretend he has married such a disreputable widow, but at least she will not burden him with feelings he can never return. She prays he will learn to tolerate her.

Alex understands his supposed wife never wishes to remarry. And if she had chosen to wed, it would not have been to him. He should have wooed her when he was whole, when he could have had her love, not her pity. But it is too late now. She looks at him and sees a broken man. He hopes she will learn to bear him.

In a masquerade of marriage, Ella and Alex soon discover they are more well-matched than they thought possible. But then the couple's blossoming trust is ripped apart by an enemy determined to destroy them both. Two lost souls must together face the demons of their past to save their lives and give their love a future.

A Baron for Becky

Becky is the envy of the courtesans of the demi-monde—the indulged mistress of the wealthy and charismatic Marquis of Aldridge. But she dreams of a normal life; one in which her daughter can have a future that does not depend on beauty, sex, and the whims of a man.

Finding herself with child, she hesitates to tell Aldridge. Will he cast her off, send her away, or keep her and condemn another child to this uncertain shadow world?

The devil-may-care face Hugh shows to the world hides a desperate sorrow; a sorrow he tries to drown with drink and riotous living. His years at war haunt him, but even more, he doesn't want to think about the illness that robbed him of the ability to father a son. When he dies, his barony will die with him. His title will fall into abeyance, and his estate will be scooped up by the Crown.

When Aldridge surprises them both with a daring proposition, they do not expect love to be part of the bargain.

Revealed in Mist

Prue's job is to uncover secrets, but she hides a few of her own. When she is framed for murder and cast into Newgate, her one-time lover comes to her rescue. Will revealing what she knows help in their hunt for blackmailers, traitors, and murderers? Or threaten all she holds dear?

Enquiry agent David solves problems for the *ton*, but will never be one of them. When his latest case includes his legitimate half-brothers as well as the woman who left him months ago, he finds the past and the circumstances of his birth difficult to ignore. Danger to Prue makes it impossible.

A Suitable Husband (first published in November 2016 in *Holly and Hopeful Hearts*)

As the Duchess of Haverford's companion, Cedrica Grenford is not treated as a poor relation and is encouraged to mingle with Her Grace's guests. Perhaps among the gentlemen gathered for the duchess's house party, she will find a suitable husband?

Marcel Fournier has only one ambition: to save enough from his fees serving as chef in the houses of the *ton* to become the proprietor of his own fine restaurant. An affair with the duchess's dependent would be dangerous. Anything else is impossible. Isn't it?

Coming soon

Concealed in Shadow

The story of Prudence and David continues in *Concealed in Shadow*.

When Prue disappears with David's half-brother, he is determined she must have met with foul play, whatever interpretation Aldridge might put on it. But finding her again may mean choosing between his country and his woman.

Here are the first three paragraphs.

The ship had been at harbour for four days now, after a stormy passage from London. The sailor who brought their daily allocation of food and drink would not answer questions, but Prue guessed they were docked somewhere in Ireland. Certainly, the polyglot shouting that filtered into the ship's hold had been flavoured these last few days with the musical lilt of Gaelic, and of Irish-intoned English.

She and Gren were shackled to the same wall bolt, with enough play in the chains that they could reach the narrow bed, the bucket that did for amenities, and the food and drink their jailors periodically sent.

They had not seen those jailors since the day of their capture. Were Wharton and Jo Palmer still aboard? Had Aldridge raised the alarm? Would David be able to find trace of them? Prue fretted away the long hours wondering.

The Realm of Silence: Book Three of *The Golden Redepennings*

Susan Cunningham's carefully managed life spirals out of control when her daughter Amy disappears from a select ladies' academy in Cambridge. Susan will do anything to find the missing fifteen year old, even accept help from Gil Rutledge, who once made her childhood miserable and yet stirs her as her deceased husband never did.

Gil seizes the chance to pursue the runaway schoolgirl up the Great North Road. It's a holiday from suffocating responsibilities he never wanted and is ill-prepared to manage—care of his mother and sisters, his dead brother's bankrupt estate. Most of all it's the chance to spend time with the only woman he has ever loved.

Catching up with Amy is merely the start. To save her, Susan and Gil must stand together against French spies and prisoners of war, English radicals, the British army and navy, and their own families. And even risk their hearts.

The Bluestocking and the Barbarian (first published in November 2016 in *Holly and Hopeful Hearts*)

James must marry to please his grandfather, the duke, and to win social acceptance for himself and his father's other foreign-born children. But only Lady Sophia Belvoir makes his heart sing, and to win her, he must invite himself to spend Christmas at the home of his father's greatest enemy.

Sophia keeps secret her tendre for James, Lord Elfingham. After all, the whole of Society knows he is pursuing the younger Belvoir sister, not the older one left on the shelf after two failed betrothals.

The Bluestocking and the Barbarian is Book 1 in *Children of the Mountain King*

With Mariana Gabrielle

Never Kiss a Toad

[A Victorian romance continuing family stories begun in the various Regency books of Jude Knight and Mariana Gabrielle.]
David "Toad" Northope, heir to the Duke of Wellbridge and rogue in the mould of his infamous father, knows Lady Sarah "Sal" Grenford, daughter of the once-profligate Duke of Haverford, will always hold his heart.

But when the two teens are caught in bed together by their horrified parents, he is sent away to finish school on the Continent, and she is thrown into the depths of her first London Season.

Can two reformed rakes keep their children from making the same mistakes they did? The dukes decide keeping them apart will do the trick, so as the children reach their majority, Toad is put to work at sea, learning to manage his mother's shipping concern, and Sal is taken to the other side of the world, as far from him as possible.

How will Toad and Sal's love withstand long years of separation, not to mention nasty lies, vicious rumours, attractive other suitors, and well-meaning parents who threaten to destroy their future before it has begun?

(*Never Kiss a Toad* is being published one episode at a time on Wattpad, and will be published complete as an ebook some time in 2017 or 2018.

Connect with Jude Knight

Jude Knight has always loved telling stories, mostly for the benefit of children in need of entertainment. Her strong determined heroines, heroes who appreciate them, and villains you'll love to loathe first made their way into the covers of a book three years ago. A dozen books later, the wind fills her sails and many more plots jostle for daylight.

Follow Jude on Twitter: @JudeKnightBooks
Friend Jude on Facebook: facebook.com/judeknightbooks
Subscribe to Jude's blog: judeknightauthor.com
Subscribe to Jude's newsletter:
judeknightauthor.com/newsletter/
Follow Jude on Goodreads: www.goodreads.com/judeknight